John Rowe Townsend

ROB'S PLACE

VIKING KESTREL

VIKING KESTREL

Penguin Books Ltd, Harmondsworth, Middlesex, England
Viking Penguin Inc., 40 West 23rd Street, New York, New York 10010, U.S.A.
Penguin Books Australia Ltd, Ringwood, Victoria, Australia
Penguin Books Canada Limited, 2801 John Street, Markham, Ontario, Canada L3R 1B4
Penguin Books (N.Z.) Ltd, 182–190 Wairau Road, Auckland 10, New Zealand

First published 1987

British Library Cataloguing in Publication Data

Townsend, John Rowe
Rob's place.
I. Title
823'.914 [J]   PZ7
ISBN 0–670–80998–5

Printed in Great Britain by
Richard Clay Ltd, Bungay, Suffolk

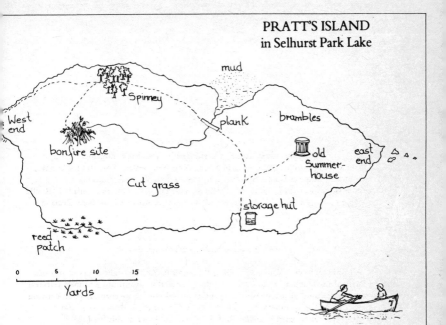

PRATT'S ISLAND
in Selhurst Park Lake

mud

Spinney

plank

brambles

West end

bonfire site

old Summer-house

east end

Cut grass

storage hut

reed patch

0   5   10   15

Yards

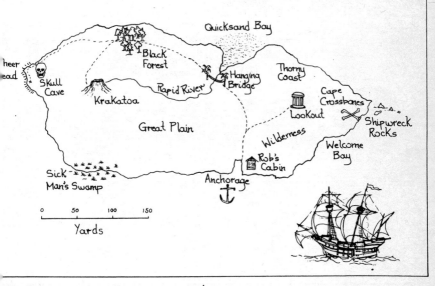

PARADISE (*or Perilous*) ISLAND
in the Pacific Ocean

Quicksand Bay

Black Forest

heer ead

Skull Cave

Thorny Coast

Krakatoa

Rapid River

Hanging Bridge

Cape Crossbones

Lookout

Shipwreck Rocks

Great Plain

Wilderness

Welcome Bay

Sick Man's Swamp

Rob's Cabin

Anchorage

0   50   100   150

Yards

I

Half-way through the summer holidays, Rob's friend Wayne left Selhurst. The removal was on a Saturday morning, and was quite exciting. Wayne's dad had rented a truck and brought it round the night before. By the time Rob got to Wayne's house, soon after breakfast, everything was in full swing. Wayne's dad and elder brother had loaded the cooker and fridge, and were struggling with the washing-machine. Wayne's mum and sister were carrying out piles of bedding and curtains. There were tea-chests dotted around and rolled-up carpets propped against the wall of the house. Everyone was bustling about and shouting at everyone else.

Rob and Wayne enjoyed themselves, fetching and carrying things and dodging out of the way of heavy pieces of furniture and being shooed away by the grown-ups and thundering round the house making the bare floorboards echo. They did a useful job, rounding up the cat and shutting it in its basket, receiving a couple of scratches each as battle-scars. By midday the loading was finished. The last cups of tea were drunk. Rob gave Wayne a battered copy of *Moonfleet*, his best-loved adventure story, as a parting gift, and Wayne gave Rob a model Spitfire that he'd assembled himself.

The Allison family divided themselves between the truck and Mr Allison's battered Cortina. Rob's last sight of Wayne was of a hand waving from the passenger side of the truck's cab. Then it was all over, and Rob was standing in the street by himself, holding a scrap of paper on which Wayne had written his new address. And it was just beginning to sink in that Wayne had gone for good, to a city a hundred miles away. This afternoon and tomorrow and next week, Wayne wouldn't be around. There would only be Mum and Keith and the baby, and on Saturdays Dad.

At least it was Saturday today. Dad would be coming this afternoon, and they could go down to the boats on Selhurst Park Lake and see Rob's remaining friend, the attendant, Mike. Meanwhile there was Saturday dinner, and it was dinner-time now.

Rob trudged home. He was hungry. Furniture-removing was hard work. In the old days, when the family was Mum and Dad and Rob, the table would have been laid, and there'd have been a good smell of cooking, and Mum would have said, 'Wash your hands and sit down, love, it's just ready.' But today there was nobody in the living-room at all. No smell of food, but a faint damp odour of the baby's washing. Rob slammed the door gloomily behind him.

Mum's voice floated down from upstairs: 'That you, Rob?'

'Yes.'

'I can't come now, I'm feeding Helen.'

'You're always feeding Helen.'

'Babies have to be fed. If *you* were a baby you'd want to be fed, wouldn't you?'

'I'm *me* and I want to be fed. Where's my dinner?'

8

'Stop this shouting-match, Rob. It disturbs Helen. You can look after yourself, you're big enough. Heat up a can of beans.'

'Bloody Helen!' muttered Rob to himself. Then he felt mean. Helen was his sister, after all. Or his half-sister, to be exact. Helen was Mum's and Keith's baby, not Mum's and Dad's.

Keith was all right. He was perfectly kind to Rob. But there was all the difference in the world between your real dad and a stepfather. And that difference cut both ways. Rob knew quite well that for Keith there was an equal difference between his own baby and his stepson. There was a look in Keith's eyes when he played with Helen that would never be there for Rob.

Rob opened a can of beans, dropped the shiny disc from the top of it into the garbage bin, and looked gloomily at the can's contents. He couldn't be bothered to heat them. He found a spoon, scooped out beans, and swallowed them cold. They weren't very nice cold, and he was still hungry when he'd finished. A new thought occurred to him. He went to the foot of the stairs and yelled, 'Can I go for some chips?'

'I told you, don't make all that noise! Yes, you can. Bring some for me as well. There's a five-pound note in my bag. Take it, and don't lose the change!'

Rob went to the chip shop. It was three streets away, and there was a Saturday queue. By the time he got back, Mum had come into the kitchen, holding Helen at her shoulder and patting her on the back. Helen gave a milky burp. Mum said, 'She's got plenty of wind up. I'll put her out in her pram. She'll be asleep in a minute. I hope.'

Mum and Rob sat at the kitchen table and shared the package of chips. Rob was tempted to point out the difference from old times, but he could see that Mum was tired and he managed – just – not to say anything.

'Where's Keith?' he asked.

'Keith's playing cricket today. It's an away match. They're having lunch on the way.'

This time the words of complaint came out before Rob could stop them. 'Dad didn't go off playing cricket. Dad was always at home on Saturdays.'

Mum didn't say anything to that. And almost at once thin wails drifted in from the garden.

'There she goes again!' said Mum. 'I expect I'll have to pick her up. You finish the chips.'

Rob ate up the chips. Mum came in with a crying Helen. Rob stuck his fingers in his ears. Mum walked around the kitchen, holding Helen and making crooning noises. Helen's cries began to die away. Rob ate the last chip, screwed up the paper and threw it into the bin. Then he went into the sitting-room, meaning to watch television until it was time to go and meet Dad.

There was nothing that interested him. There just wouldn't be. He went to his room, ran his eye along his bookshelf, and picked up a sea adventure story. It was a bit old-fashioned, but it was the kind of book he liked best. He'd read it two or three times before, but he became absorbed again, and it was a shock when at last he looked at the time and saw that Dad's bus was due in already.

Rob ran all the way to the coach station and arrived at the same time as the bus, which was a few minutes late.

Some twenty people got off it, but not Dad. Rob always expected Dad to be last off, because he was the kind of person who would hang back and let everyone else push past him. When the bus emptied and there was still no Dad, Rob could hardly believe it. He stepped inside the bus, half expecting to find that Dad had fallen asleep in his seat. But there was no one there. Dad hadn't come.

Rob rushed all the way home and into the kitchen. He could hear Helen, who was outside in her pram and crying again. But this time Mum hadn't heard her. Mum was sitting at the kitchen table, bent forward, with her head on her crossed arms. She was asleep. Mum had had a lot of broken nights lately.

'Mum! What's happened to Dad?'

Mum raised her head. It took her a few seconds to come round. Then she said, 'Oh, *no*! Not *again*!' and went into the garden. Rob followed.

'Mum! I said, what's happened to Dad?'

Mum rocked the pram gently to and fro. Then she said, 'Rob, I'm sorry! I forgot to tell you. Your dad rang up this morning while you were out. He's not coming today.'

'He's not coming today? But he *always* comes on Saturdays!'

'That's what he said.'

'Fancy forgetting to tell me that!'

'I've told you, Rob, I'm sorry.'

'Why isn't he coming?'

'He did explain, but I didn't quite take it in. He had to see somebody, I think.'

'On Saturday afternoon! Why?'

'Now listen to me, Rob Little! *I'm* not responsible for what your dad does or doesn't do. It's up to him, isn't it? I've said I'm sorry I forgot to tell you, but there's nothing I can do about it.'

The endless emptiness of a Saturday afternoon without Dad or Wayne stretched ahead of Rob. He couldn't bear the thought. Even school would have been better.

'What am I supposed to *do*?' he demanded.

Helen was tuning up again. Mum jogged the pram. 'She just *has* to be tired,' she said. 'She was awake half the night, and she hasn't slept much this morning . . .'

'I said, what am I supposed to do?'

'I can't keep you entertained, Rob,' said Mum wearily. 'I've enough to cope with, never mind that!'

'Other people's parents *take* them to places.'

Mum looked for a moment as if she could have hit him. But she didn't. She said, in a tone of voice that was trying hard to be patient, 'What would you have been doing if your dad had come?'

'Going to the boats,' said Rob promptly.

'Well, you can go to the boats by yourself. I don't suppose you'll come to any harm. The boats on the children's pool are supervised, aren't they?'

'It costs fifty pence for half an hour.'

'Bring me my handbag.'

Rob fetched the handbag. Mum peered into it. 'I thought I had a five-pound note,' she said.

'You did. I took it for the chips. I put the change back. Four pounds twenty.'

'Oh. Well, here's a pound. Spend it how you like. And be back for tea at six.'

Rob was on the point of saying 'I'd rather have my dad than a pound', but something warned him not to. He took the money and went. When he left, Mum was still rocking the pram and Helen whimpering.

Rob walked disconsolately down to the park. He was cross with Dad for not coming and with Mum for not remembering to tell him. And when he got to the boats there was a queue, and his friend, Mike, the attendant, was too busy even to notice him.

The children's boating pool was a roped-off corner of Selhurst Park Lake, generally known as the Big Lake. The Big Lake was a mile and a half long and nearly a mile wide. Selhurst Park had once been the home of the Dukes of Middleshire, but it had been taken over years ago by Selhurst City Council. There were tennis courts and bowling-greens and miniature golf and a bandstand and a car park and the Pavilion. And there was boating: rowing boats on the Big Lake for adults and pedal boats on the small pool for children.

Rob's friend Mike was tall and thin and red-haired. He was a student who had a summer job in the park. Mike took the money for the pedal boats, and stamped the time of issue on the tickets, and helped the children into the boats, and kept an eye on them in case they fell into the water. When their time was up, Mike would call to them through a loud-hailer to come in, and if they didn't come in of their own accord he had to wade out in his thigh-boots and haul them in. (It was no good charging them extra for being late, because most of them hadn't any more money.)

Mike knew Rob well and always called him 'pal'.

Mike knew Dad well, too, because Dad had so often taken Rob to the boats. Mike always called Dad 'Dad', which made him seem to Rob like a kind of elder brother. Rob thought Mike was great.

More often than not in the last few weeks, Wayne had come to the boats with Rob and Dad. Then Rob and Wayne could share a boat, sitting side by side. This was more fun than being on your own, because both of you could pedal, and Rob and Wayne together could get round the pond faster than anyone else.

When Wayne came out with them on Saturdays, Dad would pay for him and would take them both for a meal in the Pavilion. The days when Wayne didn't come, Rob would be disappointed. But Dad would have more money to spend, because of not having to pay for Wayne. Then Dad would take Rob out for an hour in the full-size rowboats on the Big Lake.

In the middle of the lake was a humped and wooded island, thirty or forty yards long. There were signs on both sides of the island saying LANDING STRICTLY FORBIDDEN. PENALTY TEN POUNDS. BY ORDER, J. TIMMINS, TOWN CLERK. Rob would have liked to land on the island, in spite of the notice. But Dad couldn't risk a fine of ten pounds. It was as much as he could afford to come to Selhurst each week on the coach, without paying fines.

And this week Dad wasn't here. Ahead of Rob was a straggly, squabbly line of eight or ten children, waiting for boats to come in. Among them were Colin Baxter and Tim Weatherall, who were the biggest boys in Rob's class at school. Rob didn't like Colin at all. Tim was all right on his own, but when he and Colin got together they fooled around, teased other children and sometimes bullied them. Tim and Colin got Boat Number Nineteen, and five minutes later Rob got Number Nine.

Rob pedalled his boat round the pool. He'd reached the farthest point from the ticket booth when Tim and Colin, working furiously at the pedals, overtook him and penned his boat against the railings. Rob tried to back out, but they backpedalled faster than he could, and stopped him again. Colin dipped his hand in the water and splashed Rob. Rob tried again to escape, and again they were too quick. Both of them began splashing him.

Then Mike was on the bank with his loud-hailer. 'Number Nineteen!' he was calling. 'Leave Number Nine alone, or you'll come straight in!'

Tim made a rude sign with his fingers in Mike's direction, and Colin hissed at Rob that they'd get him afterwards, but they left him alone all the same. They knew that if they didn't, Mike would bring them in whether their time was up or not. That was in the rules.

Rob pedalled slowly and dispiritedly round the pond. It wasn't much fun on his own, and he was still depressed. Everyone seemed to be against him, even his classmates. When his half-hour was up, he sat down again on the bank, close to the ticket booth. He couldn't see Tim or Colin anywhere around, but he wasn't taking any chances.

The queue for pedal boats had dwindled by now. After a few minutes, Mike had time to chat with Rob.

'You're looking fed up today, pal,' he said.

Rob didn't feel like denying it.

'Where's your dad?' Mike went on.

'I don't know where he is,' said Rob. 'He hasn't come today.'

'Doesn't often miss, though, does he?' Mike said. 'I seem to see him every week, just about.'

'He never misses,' said Rob. 'At least, he never missed before.' He felt very sorry for himself.

'Too bad,' said Mike. And then, 'Like to help me for a bit? If you've nothing else to do.'

Rob brightened. He'd sooner be helping Mike than hanging around for the next couple of hours. 'All right,' he said.

'You can mark up the board,' Mike told him.

It was an old-fashioned system. Nothing electronic about it. On the outside wall of the ticket booth was a blackboard with the numbers of all the boats from one to twenty-four printed down the left-hand side of it. When Mike issued a ticket, Rob chalked opposite the boat's number the time it was due in. There was a clock in the booth, and when time was up Rob told Mike and Mike called the boat in. Then Rob rubbed out the time on the board, ready for the boat to go out again.

After a while, Mike had time for another chat with Rob.

'What about your friend?' he inquired. 'What's happened to *him*?'

'He's left,' said Rob glumly.

'For good?'

'Yes. They've gone to Newcastle.'

It was a long way to Newcastle. Wayne might just as well have gone to the North Pole.

'You're having a hard time, pal, aren't you?' said Mike with sympathy. 'What can I do to cheer you up?' And, after a minute, 'How'd you like a trip on the rescue boat?'

That was a magnificent offer, and Rob's spirits rose at once. The rescue boat had an outboard motor, and was the only powered vessel allowed on the lake. It was moored close by the landing-stage where rowboats were hired, and it hardly ever went out, because people hardly ever got into difficulty on Selhurst Park Lake. The very thought of a ride in the rescue boat was exciting.

'When?' he asked.

'Tomorrow morning, early. The boats don't open till ten o'clock, Sundays. I have to go over to the island before that, to cut the grass. I could take you with me without anybody knowing. How about it, Rob? Could you get down here about half past eight? Would you be allowed?'

'Oh, I'll be allowed all right,' said Rob. 'Nobody cares where I am. All they care about is the baby.'

'Come off it, young Rob!' said Mike. 'It's not like you to say a thing like that. And I don't believe it!'

Rob was embarrassed. He knew in his heart that what he'd just said wasn't true. If he hadn't been in a bad mood he wouldn't have said it.

'Anyway,' said Mike, 'you come here at half past eight tomorrow morning and I'll take you to the island in the rescue boat. You'll be the only kid in the school who's done that. Does it make you feel better?'

'A bit,' said Rob.

2

Keith was back from cricket by the time Rob got home. He was in a cheerful mood. Selhurst had won by eighty-four runs, and Keith had scored thirty-eight of them. Keith was a tall, active, strongly built man with black hair and a black moustache. The house, which seemed half empty when only Mum and Rob and Helen were in it, felt full to overflowing when Keith was there.

Keith was good-looking, no doubt about it. Compared with him, Dad was something of a shrimp. At nearly forty, Dad was ten years older than Keith; he was on the small side and his hair was beginning to thin. But Dad was Dad, and Rob was loyal to him. Keith had a hot temper, which sometimes got him into trouble on the sports field or after arguments in the pub, but he was patient and friendly towards Rob, and Rob would quite have liked him if he hadn't taken Dad's place in the household. Just occasionally, when Mum and Keith seemed too affectionate towards each other, Rob felt a stab of sheer hatred for Keith.

It didn't take Keith long to notice that Rob was dejected.

'What's the matter with you, lad?' he inquired. 'You look as if you'd found a penny and lost tenpence.'

Rob didn't answer, but Mum said, 'He's upset because his dad didn't come today.'

'Walter didn't come? Why?'

'Oh, some kind of business, I forget what. He rang, and I didn't give Rob the message. That made it worse, of course. But Helen was playing me up again.'

'Hard luck, Rob,' said Keith. 'A pity your dad isn't on the phone, so you could ring him yourself.'

Since the divorce, Dad had lived by himself in lodgings, in a city fifty miles away. You couldn't get him on the telephone. He had to go out to make calls.

Rob was still silent. Keith said, encouragingly, 'I expect he'll be along next week, won't he, Pam?'

'Well, he didn't say he *wouldn't*,' said Mum.

That wasn't much comfort for Rob. Next week was a long way away. Keith said, 'Hey, Rob, why don't you and me do something together tomorrow?'

'You'd like that, wouldn't you, Rob?' said Mum.

'I don't mind,' said Rob. 'But not tomorrow *morning*. I'm doing something already.'

'That's good,' said Keith. 'What?'

'I'm going to the lake island in the rescue boat,' said Rob proudly. 'One of the boat attendants is taking me.'

Mum looked dubious. 'Are you sure that's safe?' she asked.

Rob said, 'Course it is. The rescue boat won't sink. And I won't fall in.'

Mum said, 'I didn't mean that. I mean, is this attendant a person you ought to be going with?'

Keith said, 'Who is it, Rob?'

'It's Mike. I think his other name's Tindall. He's a pal of mine.'

Keith grinned and said, 'He means Mike Tisdall. Has

19

red hair, hasn't he, Rob? I've known Mike for years. He used to play football with Selhurst juniors. Mike's all right, Pam. Rob'll be as safe as houses with him.'

'Oh, well, in that case . . .' said Mum.

So on Sunday morning, with Mum and Keith still in bed and Helen quiet for once, Rob slipped out of the house and made his way down to Selhurst Park Lake. He'd timed it well. Mike was at the main landing-stage, untying the rescue boat.

'Jump in,' he told Rob. 'Prepare for the great adventure. Pratt's Island, here we come!'

'Pratt's Island?'

'That's its name. Bet you didn't know, did you? Most people don't. They just call it "the island".'

'Why Pratt?' asked Rob.

'Pratt's what the Dukes of Middleshire were called before they went up in the world.'

'It doesn't sound very exciting,' said Rob.

'Well, you and I can call it anything we like, can't we? What's it to be, Rob? You're a great one for reading. How about Treasure Island?'

'We can't call it that,' said Rob firmly. 'That's in a book.'

'Coral Island, then?'

'That's in a book, too.'

'Pirate's Island? Jolly Roger Island? Cannibal Island? Coconut Island?'

Rob shook his head at all of these. Mike said, '*You* think of something, then.' He swung the outboard motor over the back of the boat and pulled a cord to start it. In a moment they were heading out over the lake.

They hadn't far to go. It wasn't much more than a quarter of a mile to the island. Opposite the landing-stage they'd set out from was an inlet, and beside it a small wooden shed.

'That's where we're going to tie up,' said Mike. 'But you don't want your trip to be all over in two minutes, do you? Let's take a turn round the island before we land.'

He put the tiller across, slowed the engine, and steered the boat in a gentle potter round the island in an anti-clockwise direction, ten or fifteen yards from the shore. The sun had come out after early cloud, and everything ashore looked green and inviting.

'Hey, this is great!' said Rob. 'Paradise Island, that's what we'll call it. And the part we're passing is Welcome Bay.'

'Okay,' said Mike. 'You can do the naming, Rob. We're going round the east tip, now. What shall we call it?'

This end of the island was rough grass and bracken. It finished in a sharp point, at which there were two or three large stones lying in shallow water and looking as if they'd fallen off.

'That's Cape Crossbones!' said Rob instantly. 'The rocks are Shipwreck Rocks, where many brave men have drowned.'

'Okay,' said Mike again. 'What about the next bit?'

There were yards of brambles along the water's edge.

'This is the Thorny Coast,' said Rob, inspired. 'Where sailors have died trying to force their way through the tangle.'

21

'Great. And now, Cap'n?'

They were cruising along the side of the island that faced away from the landing-stage and towards the farther shore of the lake. At each end of the island was a hump of high ground, and on the hump at this end Rob could now see a small, round stone building, with a ring of slender columns instead of walls. It was invisible from the mainland, concealed by a little clump of trees.

Instead of answering Mike's question, Rob asked, 'What's that up there? I mean, what is it in real life?'

'That was the old Duke's belvedere. A kind of summer-house. He used to sit up there admiring the view, or so I'm told. Owned everything in sight. And now it all belongs to the town.'

'We can't have a summer-house on a South Sea island,' said Rob. 'Let's call it the Lookout. We keep someone up there night and day to watch out for pirates or savages.'

'Seems a wise precaution,' said Mike.

Ahead of them now was a little cove, with a narrow shore of muddy sand.

'Quicksand Bay,' said Rob.

'I don't think there's likely to be quicksands around here,' said Mike.

'*Course* there's quicksands. If you tread in the wrong place, you're up to your neck in no time. But if there was pirates after you, you might have to take a chance on it.'

A tiny trickle of water, too small to be called a stream, ran out into the cove at this point. Somebody had laid a plank across it.

'That's the Hanging Bridge over Deep Gorge,' Rob

said. 'And the river's the Rapid River. You have to watch out, in case your enemies cut one end of the bridge when you're half-way across the gorge.'

They passed a spinney of some twenty trees, which Rob named the Black Forest. But he didn't know quite what to make of the hump at the western end of the island.

'It's the old beacon site,' said Mike. 'We still light a bonfire there in autumn, to get rid of brushwood and stuff.'

'Krakatoa!' said Rob.

'Strikes me Paradise Island is a dangerous place,' said Mike, grinning. 'The real Krakatoa erupted and blew a whole island to bits. Killed thousands.'

'Paradise Island has another name,' said Rob darkly. 'Perilous Island! Sometimes it's one, sometimes the other. See that hollow under the cliff? That's Skull Cave!'

'Scene of many murders, I dare say,' said Mike.

'Yes. Dozens. That's why it's full of skulls.'

'Let's get away from it, quick!' said Mike.

They were at the western tip of the island. The cliff here was four or five feet high.

'You could twist your ankle if you fell off there,' Mike said. 'And get your feet wet, too.'

Rob looked scornfully at him. 'Twist your ankle?' he said. 'You'd break your neck if you crashed down those cliffs! Can't you see? You'd fall hundreds of feet into the sea. That's why it's called Sheer Head.'

'Sorry,' said Mike. 'I mean, Aye, aye, sir.'

They were three quarters of the way round the island now. Down from the cliff on the south side was a marshy patch, and the coastline was blurred because mud and reeds stretched out into the water.

'That's Sick Man's Swamp,' said Rob.

'Don't tell me,' said Mike. 'If there was anyone that wasn't wrecked on Shipwreck Rocks or torn to bits on the Thorny Coast or shot by pirates or sunk in the quicksands or killed by a fall off Sheer Head or murdered in Skull Cave, then he'd catch a deadly fever in Sick Man's Swamp and die of that.'

'How'd you guess?' said Rob, grinning.

'You have a bloodthirsty imagination!' said Mike.

They were nearly back at their starting-point, having circled the island. Past Sick Man's Swamp was a patch of grass, about the size of a suburban lawn. It had been kept cut, though it was a bit ragged just now.

'It's the Great Plain,' said Rob.

'And I have to mow it,' said Mike. He headed the boat into the inlet they'd seen when they first approached the island.

'And here we are at the Anchorage,' said Rob.

Mike tied the boat to a post on a tiny landing-stage. 'Well, we survived,' he said. 'Didn't get shot or drowned or eaten.'

Rob climbed ashore. The wooden shed beside the landing-stage was padlocked. Mike took a key from a bunch and unlocked it. The shed was just big enough for the two of them to get inside. In it were a petrol-driven lawn-mower, a fuel drum and some garden tools.

'This is the place to build a log cabin,' said Rob, his mind still full of South Sea islands. 'Right beside the Anchorage and not too far from Welcome Bay.'

'After all that exploration,' said Mike, 'you must be ravenous, eh, shipmate?'

Until that moment it hadn't occurred to Rob to feel hungry. But he'd come out without any breakfast, and as soon as Mike spoke he felt the pangs of an empty stomach.

'Guess I'll have to tighten my belt,' he said stoically.

'No need for that. We have our rations,' said Mike. 'Go to the boat and look under the seat at the back.'

Rob went to the boat and found a supermarket bag tucked under a seat. Mike took from it two packets of potato crisps, two pork pies and two cans of lemonade.

'Ship's biscuit, wild pig and rum,' he said. He opened a can by the ring-pull and sang in a cheerful baritone, 'Fifteen men on the dead man's chest . . .' Rob joined in, 'Yo ho ho and a bottle of rum!' They swigged lemonade and ate the food. It was soon gone.

'I'm going to tame the wilderness now,' said Mike. 'Why don't you go up to the Lookout and see if there's any pirates in sight?'

Mike got out the motor-mower and started it. Rob climbed the little hill to the old Duke's belvedere. It was a pleasant little structure, open to the air between its columns, with a circular stone bench running round most of the inside.

People had been here since the Duke's day. There were a few rude words and drawings, and the information that KILROY WAS HERE and KENNY LOVES CILLA. And there was a little row of initials crudely cut into the stone: KH, DM, WE, FC. But none of this looked very recent.

Rob liked the place. He walked round the inside, looking out between the columns. It was certainly a splendid viewpoint. Though at one side he had to squint between branches, he could with a little effort see all the island, all the lake, most of the park, and the roofs of new houses outside it. There were people walking in the park now, and dogs running around, but there weren't any boats on the lake because it wasn't yet opening time. Directly below him was Mike, mowing the Great Plain, and beyond was the other hillock that he'd named Krakatoa.

Rob felt good. He wished he could come here often and bring a friend. Wayne would have loved it. But Wayne had gone. He didn't want to think about that. He ran down the slope and joined Mike on the grass. Mike welcomed him and let him take turns with the motor-mower.

When they'd finished, Mike put the mower away and locked the shed. They got back in the boat. 'Want to take the helm, shipmate?' Mike asked. And it was Rob who steered the rescue boat back to the mainland. Mike switched off the engine as they approached, and the boat glided gently back to its mooring.

'Damn. There's Terry,' said Mike. 'He's early today.'

It still wasn't opening time, but Terry, who looked after the adult boat station and was also the foreman, had just arrived. He didn't look too pleased at seeing Rob step from the rescue boat, but he didn't say anything. Mike and Rob walked across to the children's pool.

'Well,' said Mike, 'did you have fun?'

Rob said solemnly, 'It was terrific. It was the best morning I've ever had. The best in my whole life.'

'That's good,' said Mike.

Rob said, hesitantly, 'Next time you go, could you – could you take me again?'

Mike looked embarrassed. 'Tell you the truth, Rob,' he said, 'there isn't going to be a next time. I'm leaving, the end of this week.'

Rob was horrified. 'But *why*?' he demanded.

'It's only a vacation job, Rob. I'm studying at Selhurst Polytechnic. And next week I'm off to Yugoslavia with a couple of pals, until term starts. There might be weekend work for me in the park later on, but I can't count on it. And anyway it wouldn't be on the boats. They'll have closed for the winter.'

'But, *Mike*! You *can't* go away! With Wayne gone, I haven't any friends except you. And my dad not coming this week, and everything! And then not telling me!'

Mike looked at Rob with concern.

'Maybe I was wrong not to tell you,' he said at last. 'But I didn't want to spoil it for you. I wanted you to enjoy yourself today, and you did.'

'I don't suppose I'll ever enjoy myself again!' said Rob mournfully.

'Oh, come off it, Rob! Of course you will!'

'And I won't see the island any more!'

That was a cruel blow. To have seen the island once, to have had such a splendid time, and then not to see it again – that was worse than never having seen it at all.

Mike said doubtfully, 'I could see if somebody else might take you some time. But I don't think there's much hope. Fact is, Terry doesn't like it.'

'It wouldn't be the same anyway,' said Rob. 'It was

27

going with you, and imagining things together, that was special. Nobody else would do that.'

'Well, now, Rob,' said Mike thoughtfully, 'as for that, maybe there's something you can do for yourself. Come with me along the bank.'

Children were beginning to line up at the kiosk, but it was still ten minutes to opening time. Mike led Rob fifty yards along the lakeside. Between the boat station and the Pavilion was the parking lot, at present almost empty, and between the parking lot and the lake shore was a high hedge. Mike squeezed through the hedge. Rob followed him. And where the shore formed a tiny headland there was a small secret place, most of it occupied by a huge, spreading beech tree. At the edge of the water, the tree threw a long, low arm out sideways.

'Can you climb on to that, Rob?' Mike inquired.

'Course I can,' said Rob. He scrambled on to the branch. Mike sat on it beside him. The branch swayed, but was amply strong enough to hold them.

'Now look out to sea,' said Mike.

'To sea? The sea's fifty miles away.'

'Oh, Rob, Rob!' Mike shook his head in comic dismay. 'Where's all that imagination you were showing a little while ago? The sea's right here in front of us. The Pacific Ocean.'

'The Pacific . . .? Oh, I see.'

'That's better. Now, Rob, what do you see, far away, across the ocean?'

Rob grinned. He'd got the idea now.

'Paradise Island,' he said. '*Our* Paradise Island!'

'That's it,' Mike said. 'Now, where d'you think we

are? Well, I'll tell you. We're on our yacht. Can't you feel it moving under you?'

'The swaying of the branch?' said Rob.

Mike frowned. 'What do you mean, swaying of a branch?' he said. 'Don't you know the swell of the sea when you feel it? We're out on the ocean!'

'Yes. Course we are!' said Rob, delighted.

'We're sailing for the island. There's a fresh breeze, and we're heeling over. You can feel *that*, can't you?'

'You bet I can!' said Rob.

'We'd better not capsize. There's sharks in these southern seas. And don't fall overboard, shipmate . . . There now, the water's creaming away behind us, we're doing ten knots at least. Oh, a life on the ocean wave!' Mike sang. Then, 'Can't you see, Rob? The deep blue sea all round us, the southern sun, the cloudless sky, and Paradise Island on the horizon, getting nearer, getting bigger . . .'

Before Rob's eyes, the cool grey Midland sky was transformed to a Pacific blue, the municipal lake to an ocean. Above his head were white sails, responding gloriously to the wind.

'Like to look through the telescope?' Mike asked. He mimed passing it over. Rob put it, in imagination, to his eye, and saw in close-up the vivid green and gold of a tropical island.

'North-east by north, that's our course!' said Mike. 'We'll drop anchor in Welcome Bay!'

'Aye, aye, sir!' said Rob.

Mike spoke in an ordinary voice. 'You see?' he said. 'You can always go there, if you want to enough. When you need a break you can come down here, in sight of the island, and use your imagination as a boat. You can do it, young Rob, *I* know. When I've gone, I'll think of you doing it. But just for now, I have to leave the Pacific Ocean and open up the pond for the kids.'

3

Rob spent the rest of the morning helping Mike at the children's pool, and got free time on a pedal boat for payment. Terry didn't see him, or, if he did, didn't say anything. Apart from the bad news that Mike was to leave, it was a satisfactory morning.

He arrived home to the sound and smell of frying. Keith was bending over the stove.

'Well timed, Rob,' he said, grinning. 'Dinner in five minutes. Why don't you set the table? You know better than I do where to find things . . . Did you get to the island?'

'Yes.'

'How d'you like it?'

'It was great. I wish I could go again.'

'I went there when I was about your age,' said Keith. 'Not officially, mind you. Me and two or three pals, we snuck over there from the far side of the lake, on a raft.'

'Did you?' said Rob. As often happened, he found himself at the same time quite liking Keith and yet resenting him. Somehow he wasn't pleased that Keith had got to the island before him. Keith just *would* have done that . . .

'What's for dinner?' he asked.

'Bacon and beans and sausages.'

'Sounds more like breakfast than dinner.'

'Sorry, chum. You're not at the Ritz. I cook what I *can* cook.'

'We used to have roast beef on Sundays,' said Rob. 'And Yorkshire pudding and baked potatoes.'

'The good old days, eh?' said Keith. He sounded rueful. 'I'm not quite up to roast beef and Yorkshire pud. Not yet. Maybe I'll learn. I'll have to take lessons from your mum.'

'Where *is* Mum?'

'She's having a lie-down. Helen's gone off at last. With a bit of luck your mum'll get her dinner before it all starts up again. Ow!' Keith jumped back from the stove as a sausage burst and spat fat at him. 'I guess I got the gas turned up too high. Was your dad a good cook, Rob?'

'He didn't *need* to be,' said Rob. 'My mum did the cooking.'

'Yes, well, there wasn't a baby in the house then, was there?'

'She had a job. *And* did the cooking.'

'Jobs are forty hours a week. Or less if it's part time. Babies are twenty-four hours a day, seven days a week. That's the difference. And some babies . . .'

'Are like Helen,' said Rob. 'I bet *I* wasn't.'

'I wouldn't know about that,' said Keith. 'Helen's the first baby I've had, that I'm aware of.' Then, 'We're ready to eat, Rob. Go tell your mum, will you? She's lying down, but I don't think she's asleep. And, Rob, be quiet going up those stairs. It doesn't take much to wake Helen.'

Rob went upstairs and into the bedroom that had once been Mum's and Dad's, but was now Mum's and

Keith's. Keith had thought Mum wouldn't be asleep, but she was. She was lying fully dressed on top of the bed, snoring very softly. In her cot by the bed, Helen made little snuffly baby noises. Rob leaned over the cot and couldn't help smiling at Helen for a moment. But he sternly switched off the smile and went round to Mum.

'Mum!' he began in an ordinary voice, then remembered and dropped it to a whisper. 'Mum! Dinner's ready!'

Mum opened her eyes. For a moment she looked blank.

'Dinner!' repeated Rob.

Slowly Mum swung her legs to the floor and sat on the edge of the bed, rubbing her eyes.

'I could sleep for a week,' she said.

'Dinner!'

'Yes, I know. I heard you. I'm coming. Tell Keith I'll be down in a minute.'

Keith was putting food on the plates. By the time Mum appeared he'd dished up. He and Rob waited for Mum. When she reached the table, Keith began to eat heartily. He was a big man and used a lot of energy. Rob tucked in, too. Although bacon and sausages didn't seem to him to be a proper Sunday dinner, he actually liked them better than he did roast beef. But Mum sat looking at her plate and toying with a fork.

'Is it all right for you?' Keith asked. 'Cooked right?'

'Oh, yes, fine,' said Mum without interest. 'It's just that I don't feel much like eating, somehow.'

'You've got to eat,' Keith said. 'You're still eating for two, remember.'

'Yes, I suppose so.' Mum cut a small piece off the end of a sausage and sat looking at it.

'Go on, eat up!' said Keith.

Mum began eating in a slow, picky way. Then from upstairs came a small, thin wail. Mum's eyes met Keith's.

'Maybe she'll go off again,' said Keith hopefully. Mum took a forkful of bacon. And then it began again – at first cries and silences, then a continuous crying.

Keith had emptied his plate. 'Maybe I could go to her,' he said.

'*You* can't give her what she wants!' said Mum. 'I'll go.'

'I'll put your dinner under the grill, shall I?' said Keith.

Mum got up to go out. 'It's no good,' she said in a despairing tone. 'I've no time to do *anything*. It's a wonder I even get to the loo!'

'Why did you have to *have* a baby,' said Rob, 'if you don't like it?'

Mum's temper snapped. She turned, furious, flew at Rob and boxed his ears. He backed away, more frightened than hurt.

'Hey! Hold it!' said Keith to Mum, jumping up.

Mum said, 'I have enough to cope with, without that. If I have to take that sort of thing from *him*, it's the last straw!' She turned on her heel and went.

Keith said to Rob, sharply, 'You deserved that! We can do without that kind of remark!'

'Sorry,' said Rob sullenly.

Keith said, 'I'm going after her. You stay right here. There's ice-cream in the fridge for when you've finished your bacon.'

Rob finished his meal with a dollop of pink ice-cream. He thought of washing the dishes, by way of being helpful, but decided he wouldn't. It wasn't turning out to be such a good day after all. And a long empty afternoon lay ahead of him. He switched on the television and tried all the channels in turn. There was nothing that appealed to him, but he watched a programme anyway, because he couldn't be bothered to switch off.

After twenty minutes, Keith reappeared. He had Helen over his shoulder and was patting her back, burping her.

'You dropped yourself in it that time, kiddo,' he remarked. 'Your mum was up half the night, last night and the night before. She's at the end of her tether. We must do what we can, Rob, you and me . . .'

'Mum's not the only one who's fed up,' said Rob. '*I'm* fed up. No friends, nothing to do . . .'

'I can't understand you, Rob. *I* never used to get like that. When I was a lad, we went around in a gang and we always found plenty to do. Too much, maybe. We were always in and out of trouble. But talk about being lonely and having nothing to do, I wouldn't have known what you meant. Mind you, I was always the leader in whatever we were doing. All the lads wanted to play with me. Until I took to organized sport. That kept me out of mischief, more or less. You don't go in for sport, do you, Rob?'

'Not much,' said Rob.

'And your dad doesn't, either.'

'No.'

'There's a lot of pleasure in sport, Rob.'

'It's not much fun when you aren't any good at games,' said Rob.

Keith said thoughtfully, 'Maybe we could do something about that.' And then, 'This afternoon, why don't you and I take Helen for a walk in the park while your mum rests?'

Having nothing else to do, Rob didn't object. Five minutes later the two of them set off with a sleeping Helen in the direction of the park.

Keith pushed the pram with a swagger. 'No good doing this as if you're ashamed of it,' he said. 'Not that I look like a wimp, I reckon. If anyone cares to make anything of it, I'll show them.'

At the souvenir shop beside the park gate, Keith told Rob to guard the pram for a minute. He went into the shop and came out with a white plastic football.

'It'll soon be the football season,' he said. 'And seeing Helen's asleep, let's see how you shape up.'

Inside the park, Keith put the brake on the pram, dropped the ball to the ground, dribbled it a few yards, and invited Rob to take it from him. Rob attempted a tackle. Keith evaded it easily. Rob tried again and failed again.

'All right,' said Keith. 'Now you have the ball and I'll try and take it from you.'

Rob dribbled the ball, not very competently. Keith came up to him, extracted it effortlessly, dribbled it for a few feet, and passed it back. 'Keep trying,' he invited.

Rob kept trying. After a while Keith said encouragingly, 'You're getting better.' But Rob didn't believe it. A minute later, trying a big kick, he sent the ball in the air and it came down on Helen's pram. It bounced off again, but its impact was enough to wake Helen up, and she started to cry.

'That's torn it,' Keith said. He jogged the pram several times and made soothing noises, but the crying continued. 'I guess we'll have to pack up and go on walking. We'll practise again some other time. You'll need to improve, Rob, if you're ever going to play for Manchester United.'

'Some hope!' said Rob. '*I'll* never play for Manchester United. Or even Selhurst.'

'Well, maybe not,' Keith admitted. Then, thoughtfully, 'You're not a happy lad these days, Rob. Is there anything that'd *make* you happy?'

'If I just had a friend,' said Rob. 'Or' – with a sudden wild hope – 'a dog. If I could have a dog, that would *be* a friend. That would be great!'

Keith shook his head. Raising his voice to be heard above Helen's crying, he said, 'Nothing doing there. Your mum has all she can cope with already. How could we manage with a dog as well?'

Rob said bitterly, 'I *knew* you'd say that. I can't have *anything* I want!'

'Sorry,' said Keith, 'but you can take it from me, there isn't a chance. Now, we'd better get walking, hadn't we? See if it sends Helen off again.'

'Can I go to the boats instead?' Rob asked.

Keith said, 'To see your pal Mike? Okay, Rob, if that's what you want, off you go. I'll take Helen home.'

Rob ran down to the boat station. The children's pond wasn't very busy. Mike was talking to the head attendant,

Terry. Terry had his back to Rob, and didn't see him approach. Mike frowned. Terry turned, and frowned also. Mike made a gesture which Rob could interpret all too easily. It was telling him to go away. For some reason Mike didn't want him.

Slowly, dejectedly, head down, Rob trudged away. He was passing the car park when he remembered what Mike had said earlier in the day, as they'd sat on the beech tree branch. 'You can always go to the island if you want to enough,' he'd said. 'When you need a break, you can come down here and use your imagination as a boat.'

Well, could he? Was Mike right in saying he had the imagination? Could he make himself see what Mike had made him see, and travel alone to Paradise Island? It was worth a try.

It was still August, and although the day was grey the parking lot was almost full. Rob picked his way among scores of parked vehicles to the end near the lake where the high hedge was. He looked around cautiously before squeezing through. But the two or three motorists in sight were concerned with parking their cars and getting their passengers organized. No one was interested in him. He found the gap, slipped through it quickly, and was on the tiny headland, with the lake bank in front of him and the long branch of the beech tree stretching out level with the ground, just above his head.

Rob hooked his arms over the branch, dragged himself up, got his legs astride, and finally was seated on the branch. Then he edged his way closer to the trunk, where the branch was thicker and more comfortable to sit on. From here he could look out across the lake.

The island was less than half a mile away. Opposite him was the curving bit of shore that he and Mike had named Welcome Bay; on its right the half-submerged stones he'd called the Shipwreck Rocks. Round to the left was the inlet where he and Mike had landed. Beyond it was the notice warning people off; he couldn't read the notice from here but he knew what it said.

Everything looked disappointingly ordinary. The water was greeny-grey lake water, not the deep blue Pacific. The island was small, familiar, a bit dingy, not vivid and exciting. As he watched, a rowboat with three people aboard made its way, rather inexpertly and splashily, between his viewpoint and the island, and disappeared from view at the other side of it.

'Rounding Cape Crossbones,' said Rob to himself. He tried hard to see the boat as a sailing ship with canvas majestically spread, cleaving its way through the blue distant waters. But it remained obstinately a Selhurst Park rowboat, hired at two pounds fifty an hour and now being clumsily propelled out of sight.

Rob sighed, closed his eyes, and tried to think himself into the frame of mind in which he'd sat there beside Mike, feeling the sway of the branch as the movement of their own boat, seeing the island draw near, with the golden sands of Welcome Bay ahead. But it didn't work. When he opened his eyes, it was on the same familiar scene as before. There hadn't been any magical transformation. The trouble was that he wasn't setting out hopefully with a friend beside him. He was alone and friendless. Nobody wanted him. He couldn't even have a dog. Rob felt deeply sorry for himself. He wasn't having a marvellous adventure. It was more as if he was ship-wrecked . . .

And as the word 'shipwreck' came into his mind, he was plunged into the middle of it. Shipwreck! Instead of sitting in the beech tree, he was on board a sinking, storm-tossed vessel. Great waves pounded its timbers and poured in over the gunwales. The mainmast had crashed to the deck. Before his eyes, a sailor was swept overboard. Rob clung to a rail. The ship lurched violently. He was hurled into turbulent water, striking out, trying to swim. He was drowning. But a spar came floating past, and he was clinging to it, carried away from the doomed ship.

Ahead of him were cruel black rocks. Shipwreck Rocks! He was being washed straight on to them. He would be bruised, battered, broken, destroyed. He flung himself from the spar and struck out with all his force, struggling to get clear of the rocks. The boiling water was all around him, hurling him one way and another, sucking him under, then throwing him to the surface again. And then he was away from the rocks, and great steady pulsing waves were carrying him ashore on to a broad beach. He was gashed and bleeding and gasping for breath, but he was alive, and by sheer will power he was crawling up on to the beach, dragging his limbs from the hungry sea. He was lying on the beach, waterlogged, weary, more dead than alive. He was sleeping where he lay, sleeping the sleep of exhaustion . . .

He was waking. The sun shone overhead from a blue, blue sky. The huge waves had subsided. The sea was gentle, playful. He was on the beach of Welcome Bay – a crescent of clean, crisp sand. His clothes had dried on him and were stiff with salt. He was comfortable but a little thirsty.

He looked out to sea. Yes, there was the wreck, what was left of it. The back end of the ship – what was it called? the stern – was lodged on a spiky rock. What if there were other survivors trapped in it? Rob was a powerful and fearless swimmer. He flung off his clothes and plunged into the water. He struck out in a swift, stylish crawl, and in no time was at the wreck. There was no sign of survivors. But from somewhere out of sight came a faint, feeble whimper.

A puppy. There was a puppy in the wreck. Rob tore his way through to it, pulling out planks and beams. He freed the puppy from the timbers that were trapping it. Then, holding the puppy out of the water, he was swimming on his back for the shore. The puppy was a liver-and-white spaniel, very affectionate. It licked his face in gratitude. He and the puppy were the only survivors of the wreck.

Rob named the puppy Crusoe, and set off along the beach to explore. On the right, Cape Crossbones loomed over them. Ahead was the Wilderness, and rising behind it the hill where the Lookout stood. Farther away was the peak of the dormant volcano, Krakatoa. On shore was a rich tangle of trees and bushes, covered with vivid flowers and fruits. Coconut palms rose tall and straight to the sky.

Rob felt thirsty. He was a superb climber with no fear of heights. Swiftly he swarmed to the top of the coconut palm, and came down with a large coconut. He found a sharp stone, made a hole in the nut, and drank some of the juice. It was delicious, rather like lemonade. He gave some to Crusoe, who seemed to like it.

Turning westward now, they came to the Anchorage, a sheltered natural harbour. Here in this basin Rob decided he would keep his raft. But this reminded him that he hadn't yet got a raft. Bidding Crusoe to wait for him, he plunged into the water and swam out again to the wreck. He found some twine, and bound together the planks he'd torn out when he was freeing Crusoe. Then he looked for supplies.

There were crates of food. Cans of baked beans, cans of spaghetti, cans of sardines. Rob liked all those. There were cans of dogfood, too. That would be fine for Crusoe. And cases of Coke. Rob stacked all these supplies on the raft. He had a further look around and found a hammer, a spade, an axe, a can-opener and an assortment of tools. Finally, using a handy spar, he poled the laden raft towards the shore. As he pushed it away from the wreck, the wreck went down, lost for ever under the ocean.

Crusoe welcomed him warmly back to land. 'I am your faithful friend and you are my master,' his adoring gaze seemed to say. They had a hearty tea together, of baked beans and dogfood respectively. Rob finished his meal with a selection of brightly coloured fruits which he found growing in the Wilderness. They were all good to eat.

The sun was getting low in the sky by now, but it wasn't at all chilly. In this mild southern climate, he and

Crusoe could sleep out of doors. But what if there were dangerous animals around? That was an interesting possibility. Rob was not afraid of wild animals, however large or fierce. He would deal with them. But just now he didn't feel like getting involved. He'd done a lot already. For tonight, he would light a fire to keep them away.

He went out, with Crusoe at his heels, and gathered driftwood. There was lots of it, washed ashore from the wreck. He built his fire, starting with dry grass and twigs, and lit it. It blazed up beautifully. He and Crusoe sat together beside it. But how had he lit it? Rubbing two sticks together would be a bit laborious. Rob remembered now. There'd been a whole pack of boxes of matches in the wreck, as well as the food and the tools, and he'd brought them ashore on the raft, taking care to keep them dry.

Rob was feeling tired by now. He sat with his back to a tree, not too far from the fire. Crusoe came and jumped into his lap. Rob caressed the puppy thoughtfully. There was a lot to do when you were settling in on a desert island. Lots of things he hadn't thought of yet, but that would be fun to do with Crusoe for company. Meanwhile, in spite of the fire, it wasn't very warm after all, and sitting with his back to the tree wasn't very comfortable. He was feeling a bit stiff . . .

Rob started, and rubbed his eyes. Someone was revving a car engine rather hard in the parking lot behind him. In front of him was Selhurst Lake, and just opposite him was Pratt's Island, a scrap of land in the middle of it. A rowboat went past between him and the island.

Rob shook himself. He hadn't a watch and didn't know what time it was. He clambered down from the beech tree, squeezed cautiously through the hedge, and walked through the car park to the Pavilion, which had a clock.

Twenty past six. He was late for tea.

Would Mum and Keith be worrying about him? Rob told himself he didn't care whether they were worried or not. But the truth was that he didn't really want to worry his mum. He ran all the way home.

They were in the dining-room. Helen was awake, and crowing as Keith held her in front of him and jogged her up and down.

Mum looked relieved to see him. 'Rob, love,' she said, 'I'm sorry I hit you. It's just that I get so tired these days. I'm better now I've had a rest.' She smiled at him, a little uncertainly.

Rob said, 'It's all right.'

Helen cooed and gurgled. She loved being jumped up and down by Keith. By her dad. *She* had a dad here in the house all the time. Not fair, thought Rob; and then he felt ashamed. Helen was his sister, after all. His half-sister.

Mum said, 'You must be hungry, Rob. Shall I make you some scrambled eggs on toast?'

Scrambled eggs were what Rob liked best for tea, and Mum knew it. She'd gone out of her way to offer him his favourite meal.

'Great!' said Rob. He allowed himself to smile. He felt quite pleased with his afternoon. Thanks to Mike, he'd found a place of his own. He could go there whenever he liked. It was his kingdom and his refuge. Nobody else's. It was Rob's place. He was looking forward already to his next visit.

4

Rob mooched around the house on Monday and Tuesday, watching television and re-reading his adventure stories. The weather was cool for August, grey and showery and uninviting, and anyway he hadn't anybody to play out with. Mum was still having bad nights with Helen. Keith was on the afternoon shift and was at home in the morning, doing his best with the housework and cooking while Mum got what rest she could.

On Tuesday afternoon, when Rob grumbled to Mum that life wasn't much fun without Wayne, Mum said, 'Why don't you write a letter to him?' Rob thought this was a good idea. He wrote,

Dear Wayne, Well, here I am, never forget a promise, I said I'd write and this is it. Mike took me in the rescue boat and we landed on the island, it was great. That was the good news, now the bad news, Mike is going away too, nobody left but me. Helen still yells all the time, wish I could swap her for you, we'd have a great time, when are you coming anyway? Your old mate and fellow-criminal Robert J. Little Esquire, sounds good doesn't it but you can call me

Rob.

P.S. How are you getting on, remember me to your family and the cat.

He begged a stamp from Mum, but didn't show her the letter, because of what he'd said about Helen.

On Wednesday morning, Mum came down to the kitchen at breakfast time in her dressing-gown, having just fed Helen, and joined Keith and Rob at the kitchen table. She looked at Keith in a meaningful way, and Keith looked back at her. Then Keith said, 'Rob, we have a problem at present with Helen.'

Rob said, 'You mean, she squawks all the time?'

Keith said, 'Well, not that exactly. The trouble is, your mum's not getting the sleep she needs.'

Rob knew that already. He said nothing. Keith went on, 'It would be better if we could put Helen in a separate room.'

'Would that make her sleep any more?' asked Rob.

'It's not just when she wakes up,' said Mum. 'The fact is, I can't really sleep properly with her in the same room anyway. Babies make a noise when they're sleeping. It's not very loud, but it keeps me awake.'

'I guess mums are programmed to listen out for their babies,' Keith explained.

'But there isn't another room to put Helen in!' said Rob.

Mum and Keith looked at each other again, and then at him. And it dawned on Rob what they were planning to do.

'She's not having *my* room!' he cried.

'Well, Rob,' said Keith awkwardly, 'I don't see how we can avoid it. Like you said yourself, there isn't anywhere else.'

47

Rob was thinking hard. He said, 'Well, there's the box-room at the back of the house. Helen could have that, if you clear the junk out of it.'

Mum said, 'That's too far away. I need to be able to hear her when she *does* start crying. Your room's just right, being opposite.'

Rob stared. Keith said, 'Fact is, Rob, that box-room is where *you're* going.'

Rob was furious. His voice rose to a shriek. 'But my room's *always* been mine. I can't remember when it wasn't. You can't take it away from me. You just *can't*. I won't *let* you!'

'Now, be reasonable, Rob . . .' Keith began. But Rob didn't feel reasonable.

'It's not *right*! Everything's done for Helen. Nobody cares what happens to me.' His rage was giving place to tears. He said, choking, 'That's all I have in the world, my room. No friends, no proper dad . . .'

'What do you mean, no proper dad?'

'Well, no dad at home. *You're* not my dad!'

Keith winced. Then he said, 'I don't pretend to be your dad. But you do have a real dad, and he cares about you. It's not his fault he had to go fifty miles to find a job. And your mum's right here. And you may not believe it, young Rob, but *I* care about you, too!'

Mum said, 'Listen, Rob, I know things are hard for you. Things are hard for all of us. It isn't easy when a marriage breaks up. And I get so tired these days, Helen being what she is. But *you* don't make things any easier.'

'Oh yes, blame me!' said Rob.

Keith said, 'That's a nice room at the back there. It's as

big as the one you have now, and it looks out over the garden. Why don't we have a go at it together, you and me? We'll clear the junk out first, and then we can both decorate it. How about that?'

Rob said nothing but pulled a face.

'You can choose your own colour scheme and everything,' said Keith. 'You can have it the way you want it.'

'I don't care what colour it is or anything about it,' said Rob. 'I don't want it at all. If I can't have *my* room, you can put my things out in the garden for all I care.' He knew they wouldn't do that.

From upstairs came the sounds of Helen, starting up again. Mum said something under her breath. Keith said, 'Wind?' Mum said, 'Could be. Could be anything or nothing. Oh well, I'll go to her. Listen, it's a fine day for once. Why don't you leave the dishes and take Rob out for some fresh air?'

Keith said, 'What about it, Rob? Shall we have some more football practice?'

Rob said, 'No, thank you. I'm going out by myself.'

'Where to?'

'Down to the boats.'

'You'll be helping Mike again?'

'I expect so.'

Mum said, 'I hope he isn't being a nuisance to the attendant.'

'If he was, Mike'd send him packing,' said Keith. 'Best let him go. He won't come to any harm.' And to Rob he said, 'Go on, off you go. Here's fifty pence. We'll talk about bedrooms later.'

Helen had piped down for the moment. Mum said, 'Be back by half past twelve, Rob. And be careful.' She smiled at him, uncertainly, and held her arms open. Rob knew that if he went to her she'd kiss him. He didn't feel like being kissed. He glared at both of them, and went out without a word.

On the way to the park, he turned matters over in his mind. He'd done his best. Ever since Dad went and Keith came, he'd done his best. And it hadn't been any good. Life was worse now than it had ever been.

He had to get away. The farther he got away, the better. He couldn't bear it, the way they were treating him. They might say they cared, but their actions showed they didn't. He'd a good mind to run away. That would show them.

But Rob was a realist. The thought of running away was appealing, but where would he go? Where would he sleep? What would he eat?

He could run away to Dad, couldn't he?

To Dad, fifty miles away?

Well, there were buses every two hours. But what was the bus fare? He didn't know. It had to be a lot more than fifty pence, which was what he had in his pocket at the moment.

And if he got to Crimley, where Dad lived now, could he find Dad? Would Dad want him? After all, Dad hadn't bothered to come and see him on Saturday. And anyway, hadn't the court given Mum care and control of him? Dad would have to bring him back. There was nothing doing there.

He was approaching the lake. Maybe he'd go and talk

to Mike, though Mike hadn't seemed very welcoming on Sunday afternoon.

It was early in the day, and the children's pond wasn't busy. Mike was in one of the moored boats, mopping up water. It was a minute or two before he showed any sign of noticing Rob. Then he said, 'Won't be a minute,' and went on mopping. Eventually he swung himself ashore and walked past Rob to the kiosk. Rob followed.

'You want a boat, I suppose,' said Mike. 'How long for?'

'Hey, Mike!' said Rob. 'It's me. Rob. Your pal. Remember?'

Mike said, 'I haven't forgotten you, Rob.' He grinned apologetically. 'Truth is, Rob,' he said, 'I got into a spot of bother over you. Terry saw us coming back in the rescue boat, and told me I'd no business taking kids to the island. And then, the same day, some child's father came along complaining that I'd threatened his son and showed favouritism to you. A Mr Baxter.'

'Colin Baxter's dad!' said Rob.

'Colin Baxter was one of the pair who were splashing you?'

'Yes.'

'Well, Terry stuck up for me. Mr B. didn't get much change out of him. But he doesn't like having complaints. He said afterwards I'd better watch it. All customers to be treated alike. No special favours. I can see his point, Rob. And what's more, he's the foreman.'

'You're leaving anyway, aren't you?' said Rob.

'Yes. But I'll be looking for weekend work later in the year, so I don't want Terry against me. So there it is,

Rob. Sorry and all that, but I've to treat you as a customer like the rest. Now, you didn't answer my question. How long do you want a boat for?'

'I don't think I want one at all,' said Rob, 'thank you very much.'

'Don't be miffed, Rob. Nothing personal.'

'I'm not miffed,' said Rob, though he was, just a bit. It seemed to him that Mike was letting him down like everyone else. Anyway, pedal boats were for kids and he'd gone off them. Outgrown them. It was only because of Mike that he'd bothered with them lately. He would save Keith's fifty pence to start an emergency fund in case he did run away.

In the meantime there was only one place to go, only one refuge from an unfriendly world. He headed for the parking lot.

There were only two or three cars there, and nobody was around. Rob squeezed through the hedge, found his private spot, and swung himself up into the beech tree. From there he looked out over the lake. The day had begun fine, but it wasn't so fine now. Grey sky was reflected in grey water, and there were no boats out. But it would be warm and sunny on the island. He closed his eyes, willing himself there. Nothing happened. He looked out again, trying to transform the dreary sky to tropical blue, the town lake to the South Seas, Pratt's Island to Paradise Island. But everything refused to be transformed.

He went back in his mind to the events of his previous visit. The shipwreck, the casting-up on the shore, the rescue of puppy Crusoe . . . If he could just get back into the sequence of happenings he would be there and could continue where he left off. But still nothing happened.

The trouble was that his mind wasn't really on the island. His thoughts were still stuck in the real world. He couldn't stop thinking of the loss of his own room, the departure of Wayne, the chilly welcome he'd got from Mike. Everyone was abandoning him. It was as if he, Rob, was cast away all alone like Robinson Crusoe . . .

And then he was there. He was sitting in the sunshine on a bench made by himself, in front of his house beside the Anchorage. He'd built the house himself, too. It was a magnificent log cabin, his own and nobody else's. It was Rob's refuge, secure against wild beasts, savages and marauding intruders. He'd cut down trees, sawn logs, improvised the tools and materials he didn't have. He had made himself a chair, a table, a bed.

It had taken time, of course. He had a stick in his hand in which he was cutting a notch to mark the passage of another day. There were many, many notches in the stick. He'd been a long time on the island, all by himself. He'd been there years, in fact. He was about twenty, bronzed and fit and powerfully muscled.

In front of him Crusoe, now a mature dog, lay snoozing. Out of the bushes flew a brilliantly coloured bird, red and green and blue. Rob had tamed the bird and patiently taught it to talk.

'Hello, Rob,' it squawked in a raucous, parroty voice.

The parrot's name was Billy Bones.

'Hello, Billy Bones,' said Rob.

'Hello, Crusoe,' said Billy Bones.

Crusoe couldn't talk, of course, but he heard his name spoken. He growled gently and wagged his tail.

'Hello, Rob,' said Billy Bones. 'Hello, Crusoe. Hello, Rob. Hello, Crusoe.'

'How are you today, Billy Bones?' said Rob.

'Very well, thank you. How are *you* today, Rob?'

'I'm fine,' said Rob. 'I'm absolutely fine. This is a great place.'

'How are you today, Rob?' said Billy Bones again. He always said the same things over and over.

'Didn't you hear me, Billy Bones? I said, "I'm fine." Except . . .'

There was just one thing wrong with being the only human being on Paradise Island.

'. . . Except I'm lonely,' he finished.

'Poor old Rob, poor old Rob, poor old Rob!' squawked Billy Bones.

'I mean, you and Crusoe are great pals to me, but I need somebody my own kind as well,' explained Rob.

Then, as he looked out to sea, he saw on the far horizon a sail. It was the first sail he'd seen in all the years he'd been on Paradise Island. Rob called to Crusoe. They rushed to the beach. A small boat was coming in fast. As they watched, it was driven by the wind on to Shipwreck Rocks and broke up. Its one occupant was struggling in the water. These seas were full of sharks, but Rob didn't hesitate. He swam out with powerful strokes and dragged the newcomer ashore. He was a young man of about Rob's age, tall and well-muscled but not quite as tall or well-muscled as Rob. He was weak and gasping, 'Water! Water!'

Rob had water. He had piped it to his house from the Rapid River. The pipework was made from the hollow stalks of a giant plant, connected together. He carried the newcomer in his strong arms up to the house, and laid him gently on the bed. The young man sipped the water gratefully. 'You have saved my life,' he said, 'and I shall never forget it.'

'What is your name?' Rob asked him.

'Wayland.'

Billy Bones fluttered around. 'Hello, Wayland!' he croaked. 'How are you today, Wayland?'

Rob said, 'You remind me of a friend of mine, from when I was a boy.'

Wayland said, 'You remind me of an old friend, too.'

Rob asked, 'How did you come to be here?'

Wayland said, 'I was forced to leave my faithful old friend. Many years later I met a villain who cheated me and persuaded me to put to sea in an unseaworthy vessel that he knew would sink. Most of the crew were drowned. A few of us escaped in the ship's dinghy, but all except me died of thirst, and I put their bodies overboard. If you had not saved me, I too would be a dead man.'

Rob said, 'Was your faithful old friend's name Roberto?'

Wayland said, 'Yes!'

Rob said, 'Wayland, *I* am that faithful friend!'

Wayland said, 'Together again at last!'

Rob said, 'Welcome to my cabin! You can use it as much as you like, but it is mine and I am boss.'

Wayland said, 'That suits me fine, Roberto!' Billy

Bones flew around excitedly squawking 'Hello, Roberto! Hello, Wayland! Hello, Roberto! Hello, Wayland!'

Rob said, 'You must be starving, Wayland. Let us have a feast!' He had saved a few special things from the wreck, all that time ago, and now he brought them out to celebrate Wayland's arrival. They had a splendid feast of beans and spaghetti, and Rob opened the last can of dogfood for Crusoe.

When Wayland had rested, Rob showed him round the island. He showed him how to climb palm trees for coconuts, and Wayland did it quite well but Rob did it better. He showed Wayland how to catch and cook fish and where to find birds' eggs. They took the overgrown path that led up Lookout Hill, forcing a way through the tropical undergrowth with Rob in the lead. At the top of Lookout Hill they found the stone remains of a temple. Rob said, 'Some pagan religion has been practised here. Do you see those marks on the walls? They are blood-stains. Savages have made blood sacrifices. The island is deserted now, but some day they may come back and look for more sacrifices. That will be us.'

Wayland said, 'There's a skull and crossbones drawn here, too.'

Rob said, 'That means there have been pirates. They too may come back some day.'

Wayland said, 'I'm scared.'

Rob said, 'I'm not scared. Together we are a match for pirates or savages. But we must watch out.'

Billy Bones squawked, 'Watch out! Watch out!'

Rob said, 'And you see that peak over there? That is Krakatoa, a sleeping volcano. It may erupt any time.

Now you know why the island is sometimes called Perilous Island. We face many dangers. But trust me, and all will be well.'

They continued round the island, with Rob in the lead, Wayland following, and Crusoe coming along behind. Billy Bones had flown ahead. Then, as they were entering the Black Forest, Billy Bones came flying back, squawking, 'Look out! Look out!' Out from the undergrowth sprang a wild beast. It was a puma. It seized Wayland between its paws and was about to devour him.

Rob and Crusoe rushed at the puma, and Rob hit it with the stick he'd been using to beat down the undergrowth. The puma let go of Wayland and turned on Rob, attacking him with sharp teeth and deadly claws. Rob struggled in its grip, lost the stick, but got his bare hands to its throat.

They fought hard, rolling over and over on the ground. Crusoe would have sprung at the puma, but Rob ordered him off so that it could be a fair fight. In the end the puma cowered in front of Rob, defeated and at his mercy. Rob stood back and let it get up, then stroked its handsome head. He knew it would never attack again. He pondered whether to let it join his family. There would be himself and Wayland, Crusoe and Billy Bones and the puma. But no, he decided, the puma was a wild creature and should be left in the wild. It could go back to the forest. It would remember that he had had it at his mercy, and sometime maybe it would come to his assistance. He would call it Pumey.

The puma sidled round him like a huge cat. 'Miaouw,' it said . . .

Rob blinked. A cat had picked its way along the beech tree branch towards him and was pushing the side of its head against his hand. Automatically he rubbed its head, and it purred loudly. It was a tabby, and it had a thin red-leather collar. MAISIE, said the wording on the collar, THE PAVILION, SELHURST PARK.

Of course. Maisie was the Pavilion cat. Rob had seen her before. She butted him gently, again and again, then climbed on to his lap as if ready to settle. But Rob was stiff from sitting in the tree. He jumped down. Maisie sprang clear, suddenly lost interest in him, and wandered away.

Rob tried to switch his thoughts back to the island. But Maisie's intrusion had broken up the picture in his mind, and he couldn't make it come together again. For the time being, Paradise (or Perilous) Island was out of reach.

Oh well, he didn't mind too much. The morning's events on the island had been satisfactory, and he and his little band of comrades were poised to have further adventures. Meanwhile, it was getting on for dinner-time.

Back home, Rob found Keith in the kitchen, just beginning to fry liver and onions. His manner was friendly.

'Pity you weren't in five minutes sooner,' he said. 'I've just had your dad on the phone.'

'What did he say?'

'Says he's coming this Saturday for certain sure. So you'll be seeing him in three days' time. There, Rob, does that cheer you up?'

'Yes, it does,' said Rob. Actually it cheered him quite a lot. There'd been a fear at the back of his mind that his dad might become like Sherry Canham's dad. Sherry's dad was divorced, too. He had come to see her every week at first, but his visits had dwindled to monthly, then to occasional ones, and now she never saw him at all.

'This time your dad'll be coming to the house,' said Keith.

That was a surprise. Dad hadn't been in the house since before the divorce. Rob always met him at the bus station, and they went straight off to do whatever they were doing.

'I asked him to come,' Keith went on. 'I said, "All right, Walt, I can guess how you feel, but we're grown-up people, aren't we? We can get along together, specially if it helps Rob." That's what I said.'

Rob was dismayed. He didn't want Dad to be pals with Keith. How *could* Dad be pals with Keith? Keith had pushed him out, more or less. Not quite like that, perhaps, but that was what it amounted to. Mum had preferred Keith, and Helen was Keith's baby, and Dad had gone. Dad ought to hate Keith. He'd always supposed that Dad *did* hate Keith, though Dad never said so. Dad wasn't the kind of person to say he hated anybody.

Keith didn't notice Rob's expression. He said seriously, 'I know it's been tough for your dad, and it's tough for you, but it'll be best for us all to be on good terms. You don't mind me asking him here, do you, Rob?'

'Do what you like,' said Rob. 'I don't care.'

5

No more was said in the next day or two about Rob's change of room. He had a faint hope that Mum and Keith might have changed their minds, but it wasn't very likely. Mum was still having bad nights with Helen. On Thursday it rained all day, but Friday morning, though cool and grey, was dry. Mum and Keith were relieved when Rob announced after breakfast that he was going to the boats again.

'Still helping Mike?' inquired Keith.

It had already occurred to Rob that if he was thought to be helping Mike he could get away from the house with no more questions asked.

'Uh-huh,' he muttered.

'I reckon we owe Mike a vote of thanks,' said Keith to Mum. 'Gets the lad out from under your feet, doesn't he?'

Keith was grinning as he said it. But Rob took the remark badly. So they wanted him out of the way, did they?

'Oh, *thanks*!' he said. 'Thanks a *lot*!' And he left the house in a huff.

Half-way down from the park gates to the lake, Rob caught sight of Tim Weatherall and Colin Baxter. He thought at first they hadn't seen him. Beside the path was a glass-cased map of the park, with a pointing arrow that said YOU ARE HERE. The case was mounted on two stout posts. Rob dodged behind it. But he wasn't quite quick enough. Tall Tim and short, stocky Colin approached him in a pincer movement, one from each side. He hadn't a hope of getting away. And there was nobody within earshot.

'Hello, Rob!' said Tim, in a tone of pleased surprise. 'Fancy meeting you!'

Rob said nothing.

'Looking for something on the map, were you?'

Rob still said nothing.

'Can we help you find it?' asked Colin. 'Why don't you come along with us?'

Rob knew what that meant. They wanted to get him to a secluded spot where they could torment him in peace.

'I have to be home,' he lied desperately. 'There'll be trouble if I'm not. They'll come looking for me.'

It wasn't much of a story, especially at ten o'clock in the morning, during the school holidays. They didn't believe him for a moment. And it gave Colin an opening.

'*Who'll* come looking for you, Rob?' he inquired. 'Your dad?'

They knew his dad had gone, and Rob knew they knew. Once again he was silent.

'Or your mum's boyfriend?' Colin went on.

Rob couldn't let that pass.

'He's not her boyfriend,' he said. 'She's married to him.'

'Oh, yeah?' said Colin.

Tim said, 'She *is* married to him, Col. I saw it in the free sheet, a few months ago. SPORTSMAN WEDS, it said. It's Keith Harris. He plays cricket and football for Selhurst.'

This made Colin pause for a moment. Rob took advantage of it. 'Keith's great at sports,' he said. 'He's had offers to turn pro. And he's a big strong fellow. Anyone that did anything to me, Keith'd crunch them up!'

He thought that was probably true, but he didn't want to put it to the test.

Colin asked, in an innocent tone, 'How old's your baby sister, Rob?'

Rob didn't reply.

Tim said, 'She was born after the wedding, wasn't she, Rob?'

Rob said emphatically, 'Yes, she was!'

'But only just after,' said Tim.

Colin said, 'Was she born with a broken arm, Rob?'

Maybe Tim hadn't heard the old joke; maybe he only pretended he hadn't. He asked, 'Why should the baby arrive with a broken arm, Col?'

Colin said, 'With hanging on till the wedding-day!' He roared with laughter.

That was more than Rob could take. He wouldn't have anyone make cracks like that about his mother and sister. He struck out fiercely at Colin and caught him straight on his nose, which gushed blood. Colin staggered back. Rob felt triumphant, but he didn't stay around to enjoy his triumph. Before Tim could react he was away, racing along the path to where a dignified gentleman was pushing a lady in a wheelchair.

Rob fell into step beside him. 'Can I help you push?' he asked.

The gentleman looked surprised. 'I'm quite all right, thank you,' he said. Then he saw Tim stop short a few yards away while Colin in the background dabbed at his nose. 'There's something going on, isn't there?' he said. 'Well, you can come along with me if you need to.' And Rob, protected, walked past his enemies and out of the park. Tim made a rude gesture as he went past, and mouthed something that might have been 'Just you wait!' But it wasn't worthwhile to follow Rob into the busy street outside, where nobody could touch him.

Twenty minutes later Rob arrived by another route in the lakeside parking lot, having seen no more of Colin or Tim. He would have to watch out for them in future. But then, he'd been watching out already, or ought to have been. He wasn't all that worried.

He was angry, though. Today it was anger that fuelled his journey to Paradise Island, rather than loneliness or the wish to escape from his usual surroundings. And he had no difficulty in getting there. He didn't even have to climb into the beech tree. As soon as he was through the hedge and the island was in view, he was on the way. By the time he'd sat down under the tree, not even noticing that he was doing so, he was there with Wayland, Crusoe and Billy Bones, and in the mood for violent action.

They were on the cliff top, close to Cape Crossbones. Almost at once, Rob and Wayland saw a ship, with black sails spread, appear over the horizon. At its masthead flew the skull-and-crossbones flag, the Jolly Roger. The ship dropped anchor in Welcome Bay and two pirates, armed to the teeth, rowed ashore. One was tall, thin and sinister. The other was short, dark-haired, swarthy and ugly, and had a villainous expression. Brandishing pistols, they stumped menacingly up the beach.

Rob and Wayland knew they couldn't fight men with guns. They hid in the undergrowth, close by the cabin. The pirates stood near to them. The tall pirate said to the other, 'See that house, Collick? There are men on this island.'

The short, villainous pirate said, 'We'll murder them, Tibble, and leave their bones to be picked clean by crows and then lie bleaching in the sun.' The tall pirate said, 'Good idea. Have a swig of rum.' The pirates had brought rum ashore as well as pistols. They drank deeply from a rum bottle.

Rob and Wayland watched them. Rob was planning a campaign to defeat and capture the pirates. Unluckily, before he had time to work it out, Billy Bones flew up.

'Hello, Roberto!' he squawked. 'Hello, Wayland! How are you, Roberto? How are you, Wayland?'

That gave them away. They broke cover and ran.

'After them!' roared the first pirate.

'No! Gun them down!' roared the second.

The pirates fired their pistols. A bullet hit Wayland in the leg, and he collapsed on the ground.

'Never mind me, Roberto!' he gasped bravely. 'Make your escape!' But Rob would never leave a wounded comrade. The pirates pounded up with a rope, and gagged and bound them, regardless of Wayland's wound, which they didn't trouble to tend.

'No need to waste powder and shot on them,' said the short pirate. 'We can just leave them to die. They'll suffer all the more.'

'We must rob them first!' said the tall one.

They stole a locket that Wayland always wore, with a picture of his long-lost mother in it. Then they set off callously to explore the island.

But they hadn't reckoned on Crusoe.

Cleverly, Crusoe had lain low. When the pirates were out of sight, he ran up to Rob and Wayland and began gnawing at the ropes that bound them. Soon Rob was free. He released Wayland and removed the filthy gags the pirates had put in their mouths. He bound Wayland's wound with his handkerchief.

Wayland said, 'For pity's sake, Roberto, get back the locket with my mother's picture! It is the thing I value most in the whole world!'

Roberto tracked the pirates through the Wilderness and found them picnicking on ship's biscuits and rum. They had carelessly left Wayland's locket on the ground a few feet away. Rob crept up unnoticed and recovered it, but just as he was creeping away again he sneezed.

The pirates saw him and gave chase. Rob raced ahead of them and sped across Quicksand Bay, where he alone knew the safe points to put his feet. The pirates, thundering after him, were sucked down by the treacherous sands and sank to their knees, then their waists, then their armpits.

'Help! Help!' they cried. Heroic as always, Rob crawled out to them with a piece of timber that was lying near by, and, clutching it in turn, they were hauled to safety. But no sooner were they ashore than they villainously turned on their rescuer. Rob fought valiantly, but was one against two and was losing the battle when his friend the puma sped towards them from the forest, bore the pirates to the ground, and stood guard over them.

The pirates surrendered. Rob trussed them both up and rowed them out to their ship, where he won over a mutinous crew and finally made both pirates walk their own plank. The pirate crew hauled down the Jolly Roger and sailed away, promising to be lawful seafarers in future. Rob rowed back in triumph to Welcome Bay, where his loyal friends were waiting for him . . .

The island dissolved before Rob's eyes. He was hungry, and it must be nearly dinner-time. He was satisfied with what he'd done, and he didn't feel angry any more. But the adventure had possibilities that went beyond the paying-out of the pirates. Now he came to think of it, there was something he'd forgotten. During the fight, one of the pirates had dropped an ancient, creased, yellowing map of the island, which was undoubtedly a guide to buried treasure. On his next visit to Paradise Island, he and Wayland could go in quest of it.

He set off home, not even troubling to look around for enemies. Colin and Tim had been dealt with. He felt more contented than he'd been for some time.

His contentment didn't last. When he reached home, Helen was sleeping quietly for once, but Mum and Keith were out of temper with each other. Mum was no more pleased than Rob about Keith's invitation to Dad.

'Not that I've anything against Walter,' she was saying. 'I'm sorry for him, really. He couldn't help being . . . I don't know how to put it . . .'

'Inadequate,' said Keith.

'Well, yes, I suppose that's the word. But it's piling on the agony, asking him here. I thought we'd made a clean break. He'll just sit here the picture of misery, making me feel guilty. I'm surprised he agreed to come.'

Keith said crossly, 'Do you know, I cried off cricket for tomorrow afternoon, so I could stay in for Walter?'

'I didn't ask you to,' said Mum.

'That's what comes of acting for the best. A fat lot of thanks I get for it!' said Keith. Then he looked across at Rob and said to Mum, 'And I'll be in trouble with *him*, too. Wait for it!'

'What do you mean?' asked Rob; but his heart sank. He had a pretty good idea.

Keith said, 'I've made a start on cleaning out that room at the back, ready for you. You can help me finish if you like, tomorrow morning.'

Rob glared at him for a moment, then turned on his heel and made to stalk out of the room. Keith said, 'Don't go, Rob,' in a quiet, steely tone that had the effect of a grip on Rob's shoulder. Rob turned to face him.

'You would, wouldn't you!' he said, disgusted. 'Start it while I'm out!'

'God give me strength!' said Keith. Then, patiently, 'That's a nice room, Rob. We'll get it just right for you. We'll make it a real boy's den. You know, you're lucky.

67

When I was a lad, I had to share with two brothers, both of them bigger than me. I got the mucky end of the stick, I can tell you!'

Rob didn't say anything. Keith went on, 'If we finished clearing it tomorrow before your dad comes, we could start painting Sunday morning. Then next week we could buy some posters for the walls, maybe. There's a shop in town that sells smashing posters. Would you like that?'

'Not particularly,' said Rob.

'In fact,' said Keith, 'there might just be room for a train layout. I never had trains when I was a lad. My mum and dad couldn't afford things like that, and they wouldn't have had space for them if they *could* afford them. But we could build up a system, bit by bit . . .'

'That'd be worst of all,' said Rob, 'having *you* playing trains in *my* room!'

Keith was breathing hard. 'Listen, Rob,' he said, 'if you were *my* son, there's times when I'd be tempted to knock some sense into you.'

Rob shrugged his shoulders. He intended to irritate Keith, and he succeeded. Keith burst out, enraged, 'I've had enough of this! I'll *kill* the lad!' He was struggling with himself. Then, to Mum, 'I'm off to the Waggoners. I'll go to work from there. See you tonight.' And he was off, slamming the door.

'You had a narrow escape there, Rob Little,' said Mum grimly. 'If Keith had hit you, you'd have finished up in the Royal Infirmary, most likely. He doesn't know his own strength, specially when he loses control. For your own sake, watch it. You hear me?'

'What about some dinner?' said Rob.

'There's pies in the oven. Keith's gone without his. Oh well, he'll get food of some kind at the pub. I hope he doesn't get into any arguments there, that's all, the state of mind he's in just now . . . What are you going to do this afternoon, Rob?'

'Go to the boats.'

'You'll be lucky. It's raining again.'

So it was. Rob hadn't noticed.

'Looks like it's set in for the day,' Mum added.

'Then I'll watch telly,' said Rob. But just as he was settling down in front of it, Keith reappeared.

'Sorry, love,' he said to Mum. 'Sorry, Rob. I went over the top a bit, I guess. Must be the weather. It depresses you, a wet August.'

'I think it's the climate inside,' said Mum ruefully. But she was smiling; and suddenly she and Keith were hugging each other, hard. Rob didn't want to look, but couldn't help doing so.

'Go on, you dreadful fellow, you'll be late for work!' said Mum; and Keith embraced her again.

Rob turned to the television and stared stonily at the screen, aware of nothing but a hard lump of hate somewhere in the middle of him.

—— 6 ——

Dad was last off the bus, as usual. He came down the steps behind everyone else, grinning apologetically. He hurried over to Rob and hugged him close.

'Sorry about last week, son,' he said.

'What happened?' asked Rob.

'Didn't they tell you? I was fixing up a new place to live. A pity it had to be Saturday afternoon, but you have to go when you can. I couldn't afford to stay in digs any longer. I've got a bedsit now.'

Rob said nothing.

'It's very nice, really,' said Dad, as if Rob had criticized it. 'I've seen much worse.'

'And you're coming to the house today!' said Rob.

'Yes, well, Keith asked me. I couldn't refuse, could I?'

Again Rob didn't say anything. But he thought his silence and his expression would give Dad the message, and they did. Dad said, 'Well, it's only for once. And we might as well all be on good terms.'

That was almost exactly what Keith had said.

There'd been several showers in the morning, but the sun was shining as they walked from the bus station to Rob's house. Dad hesitated at the front door, uncertain whether to ring the doorbell or just go in. Not long ago it had been *his* house, thought Rob. But while they were on the step, the door opened and Keith was there, smiling.

70

'Come right in, Walt!' he invited.

Rob scowled. Nobody ever called Dad 'Walt'. He was always Walter.

They went into the sitting-room. Mum had been putting Helen out in her pram, and now she came into the room. She looked embarrassed. So did Dad.

'Hello, Walter,' Mum said awkwardly.

'Hello, Pam.'

They stood looking at each other. What were they going to do? Not kiss, Rob decided. Would they shake hands? But that would be silly. They'd been married to each other for twelve years, until a few months ago. In the end, they didn't do anything.

'Sit down, Walt!' said Keith heartily.

Dad sat on the edge of the sofa. Keith planted himself firmly in his chair. It was the chair that had always been Dad's.

'Would you like a cup of tea, Walter?' asked Mum.

'Or a beer?' said Keith. 'Go on, have a beer, Walt!'

Dad had never been much of a beer drinker, but this time he accepted beer. Keith went to fetch it. There was a silence. Mum said, 'Showery today, isn't it?'

'Yes,' said Dad.

'Did you have a good trip across?'

'It was all right,' said Dad.

'The bus was pretty well on time, wasn't it?'

'It left five minutes late,' said Dad. 'But it made it up along the way.'

The silence was resumed. It seemed as if Mum and Dad didn't know what to say to each other. Keith came in with bottles and glasses. Dad sat, awkwardly holding his glass, on the very edge of the sofa. Rob wondered how long it would be before he and Dad could get away.

Mum asked, 'Did you find anywhere to live, Walter?'

Dad told them about the bedsit. It was nothing special, he said, but it was convenient for his work and he wouldn't have to pay anything in fares.

'Got everything you need, has it?' said Keith.

'Well, most things. It doesn't have a TV. Maybe I'll rent one.'

Keith said, 'There'll be Saturday sport on now.'

Dad said, 'We used to watch Saturday sport in the old days.'

Mum said sharply, 'Well, *you* did. It's about all you did.'

Keith said peaceably, 'There, there. Chaps do watch sport, more than women do. Me, I'd rather play.' Rob wondered if Keith would tell Dad he'd cancelled his game today, but he didn't. 'But if I'm not playing, Walt, I always watch it.'

Keith was fingering the remote control of the television. 'We could just have five minutes of it,' he suggested. 'See what's on, anyway.'

'Keith!' said Mum. 'Walter didn't come here to watch TV!'

'Look outside!' said Keith.

Rain was crashing down.

'You don't expect them to go out in this, do you?' Keith asked. 'Sit down, Walt. No point in getting wet through. You might as well be comfortable.'

Dad shot a look at Rob. Rob looked stonily at the

wall. Dad said, 'Thanks, Keith. We'll stay just for a few minutes, till the rain stops.'

The two men settled in front of the television. Mum disappeared into the kitchen, not looking too pleased. Rob sat on the sofa beside Dad. On the screen was a county cricket match, with extremely slow scoring. Cricket was followed by tennis. Rob watched Keith's and Dad's eyes swivelling in unison from side to side.

After a few minutes the rain stopped.

'Dad!' said Rob.

'Eh?'

Rob pointed out of the window. There was sunshine on the garden now. 'Are we going out?' he asked.

'Oh. Yes,' said Dad. 'In a minute.'

Keith said, 'Have another beer, Walt!'

'Well, I shouldn't really,' said Dad. Keith opened another bottle and poured beer into Dad's glass.

'Dad!' Rob protested. 'I want to go out!'

'Give your dad a chance!' Keith told him. 'He's been working all week, and then a bus journey. It'll do him good to relax.'

Rob did his best to be patient. But he wanted his dad to himself, away from Keith. The tennis was followed by racing, with a ferociously gabbled commentary that rose to a climax as the horses swept past the post.

'Dad!' said Rob again.

Dad moved to get up, then sat down again.

Suddenly Rob couldn't stand it any longer. 'I'm off!' he said, and flounced out of the room.

In the hallway he paused. Dad had jumped up and followed him. But Keith followed in turn, laid a hand on

73

Dad's arm, and said something quietly that Rob couldn't hear. Rob went out through the front door and slammed it behind him. At the corner of the street he waited. Surely Dad would come after him. But a quarter of an hour passed. No Dad. He was still in the house with Keith.

It was all Keith's fault. The whole idea of bringing Dad here had been Keith's, and now Keith was hanging on to him, keeping him from his son. That was just the sort of thing Keith would do. He hated Keith.

Rob hung around for another five minutes, but Dad didn't emerge. Well, he wasn't going to wait any longer. But he wouldn't go back to the house with his tail between his legs. Oh, no. He stalked off down the street and, without even thinking about it, headed for the park. He went down to the parking lot and through the gap in the hedge to the beech tree.

It was no trouble at all to get to Paradise Island. He hardly even had to think about it. He was there at once, sitting in the sunshine in front of the log cabin, his own place. Billy Bones flew towards him, squawking, 'Hello, Rob. How are you, Rob? Hello, Rob. How are you, Rob?'

Wayland and Crusoe were just as glad to see him. But Rob wasn't in the mood for company today. 'I need to be on my own,' he told Wayland.

'Yes, of course, Roberto,' said Wayland. Wayland always respected Rob's decisions. Whatever Rob said, went.

Rob strode away and climbed the hill to the Lookout.

Here on Paradise Island he was monarch of all he surveyed. Wayland would do his bidding. Crusoe was his dog and Billy Bones was his parrot. He had defeated the pirates and tamed the puma. He had built his house, cleared his patch of land. He could climb and swim superbly. He could do anything.

He was terrific. Oh, he was terrific. Roberto the Great of Paradise Island. He walked round the Lookout, surveying each corner of his realm. The log cabin, where Wayland, Crusoe and Billy Bones awaited his return. Quicksand Bay, where he had rescued the treacherous pirates. Krakatoa, from which rose a tiny wisp of smoke. Beyond it, Sheer Head . . . and surely over there he saw something move? A human figure, no doubt about it. Another intruder on his island?

Rob hurtled down from the Lookout and raced towards Sheer Head. By the time he arrived, there was no sign of the mysterious figure. But he knew his eagle eye had not been mistaken. He sought around among the rocks below Sheer Head until he found an opening, barely visible except from the sea. The opening led to a large, skull-shaped cave. Skull Cave. Fearlessly, Rob entered it. It wasn't dark inside, though there were shadowy corners, because light came in through two openings like eyes in the cliff face.

Rob shouted 'Hello-o-o!' and his voice echoed eerily round the cavern. Nobody answered. But Rob perceived that there was somebody hiding in the shadows.

'Come out into the light,' he said, 'and let me have a look at you. Don't be afraid!'

Outside in the daylight, he saw that the person he'd found was a man, small and thin, with a haggard face and an air of having suffered greatly.

'Who are you?' Rob asked.

The man said, 'My name is Dag. Once I was a seafarer, the captain of a proud ship. But the owners appointed a new first mate, who stole my wife from me. Then he marooned me on this island. He is stronger than I am – a ruthless giant of a man – and I am helpless against him.'

Rob asked, 'Where are they now?'

'They sail together in the ship that once was mine. And here am I, a castaway. There is no one on earth to care for me.'

Rob said, '*I* will care for you.'

Dag said, 'You are young enough to be my grown-up son. And if I had a son, I would wish him to be just like you.'

Rob said, 'I will be your son. And some day I will see that the villain gets his deserts. In the meantime, come with me and join my happy band.'

Back at the log cabin, Rob introduced Dag to Wayland, Crusoe and Billy Bones. Wayland said, 'Dag, I will be like a second son to you.' Crusoe licked Dag's hand. Billy Bones squawked, 'Hello, Dag! Welcome, Dag!'

Dag said, 'Here, with you, I will enjoy such happiness as remains for me.' He smiled bravely. Rob said, 'Now you are one of us and we will feast together in celebration, on freshly caught fish and delicious fruit.'

But Rob himself was not completely happy. He knew there was no way to give back to Dag what Dag had lost. They were both marooned, even if marooned together.

And there was something not right. There was something he'd done that he shouldn't have done. What was more, there was something he should be doing, and doing now. A worry from a different world was breaking into his island surroundings, like a worry from waking life breaking into a dream.

The blue of the tropical sky was turning to grey, and the air was beginning to cool. Rob was sitting on the bank of Selhurst Park Lake, beside the beech tree. He had run away from his dad, who would be worried. He must go back at once.

Rob picked himself up and set off at a run through the parking lot and back towards his home. He felt sick in the pit of his stomach. A little way outside the park gates, he saw Keith. Keith was coming along the street towards him, stopping at each intersection to look both ways. When his eyes fell on Rob, he hurried forward.

'There you are!' he exclaimed, and his note of relief was followed by one of anger. 'What do you mean by running off like that? What sort of state do you think your dad's in?'

Rob said sullenly, 'Why didn't you let him come with me? That's what he was in Selhurst *for*, to go out with me.'

Keith said, 'I kept him for a minute. There was something I wanted to say to him about *you*.'

'Why should you talk to him about me? With me not there?'

Keith sighed. 'I do my best for you, lad,' he said, 'and it doesn't seem to have much effect. I don't know why I keep on trying. But I do. I've told your dad, I'm planning to take a week off work next week and give some time to you. And he thanked me for it. But as for you, Rob, you just make things harder all round. You know your dad's the worrying kind. You should have more sense than to run away. It's time you learned to act like your age!'

Rob said, 'I didn't mean to worry Dad.' But it didn't sound convincing, even to him. Keith said, 'Anyway, we'd better look for him now. He went that way. Keep your eyes peeled.'

It took them a quarter of an hour to find Dad, and when they found him he was too relieved to be cross. But Keith was cross enough for two.

'What an afternoon!' he said. 'I'm sorry about this, Walt. I guess it wasn't such a good idea of mine after all. I bet he doesn't run away when there's just the two of you, does he?'

'No, he doesn't,' said Dad. 'But it's not your fault, Keith. I just can't understand the lad.' He shook his head. 'He's a good boy at heart.'

'I dare say he is,' said Keith, 'but, God, he can be difficult!'

'Well,' said Dad, 'you must deal with him as if he was yours and punish him if he deserves it. You hear that, Rob? I won't have you taking advantage of Keith. But, oh, I'm surprised at you. It upsets me, it does really!'

Keith said, 'I'd better get home and tell Pam we found him. Will you come back to tea with us, Walt?'

Dad said, 'It's kind of you, Keith, but I'd like a little time on my own with Rob.'

'Yes, sure, I understand.'

'Thanks for everything, Keith. Glad I've got to know you better.'

'Same here,' said Keith. 'See you later, Rob.'

Dad took Rob for tea at a café in the town, and by the time they'd finished he had to go for his bus. On the way to the bus station he said to Rob, 'That wasn't a success, was it? But we're all doing our best for you. Next week Keith's planning to take you out a few times. And on Saturday, Rob, why don't you come over to Crimley and see *me*? There's somewhere for you to come to, now I've got the bedsit. And it seems to me a day away from Selhurst will be a change for you *and* them.'

'All right,' said Rob. 'If Keith's going to be off work all week, I expect I'll have had enough of him by Saturday. More than enough.'

'I wish you wouldn't talk that way.'

Rob said, 'I hate Keith. And so should you, after what he's done to you.'

For once, Dad spoke sharply. 'We'll have no more of *that*!' he said, in a tone of voice that shut Rob up. Then Dad sighed and went on, 'Here's the money for your bus fare to Crimley.'

Rob took it silently. The bus came in. Dad said, 'Goodbye, son. See you next week.' Suddenly Rob ran to him, hugged him, and wouldn't let go until the bus was on the point of leaving.

On the way home, Rob felt guilty. He wished he hadn't upset Dad. And he didn't really hate Keith. At least, sometimes he did but most of the time he didn't. He didn't know why he'd acted as he did. There were times when he didn't know what he was going to do until he did it, and then he usually wished he hadn't.

7

The next week was an up-and-down one for Rob. Keith was off work, and giving Rob most of his time. And at least Rob wasn't bored. The truth was that Keith was livelier company than Dad, and spent money more freely. He had, Rob knew, more money to spend. His job was better paid than Dad's.

No more was said about Rob's change of room. Keith hadn't got far with clearing junk from the back bedroom, and he didn't do anything more about it. Rob hoped against hope that the idea had been given up.

On Monday Keith took Rob to Pool-on-Sea, where they spent the afternoon at the Pleasure Beach. This was fun, but Keith treated Rob rather too freely to Cokes and ice-creams and portions of chips, with the result that unpleasant things happened in Rob's interior, and much of Tuesday was spent on the sitting-room sofa, watching television and making hurried trips to the bathroom. On Wednesday Rob was better, and Keith took him to watch a one-day cricket match at the county ground. This was quite a success, with some fast scoring and a narrow win in the last over for their own county. Rob got almost as excited as Keith.

On Thursday, a beautiful day, they all went for a picnic in the country. Mum packed a splendid lunch, with cold chicken and pork pie and ham sandwiches. It was a bit of an ordeal for Mum herself, who had to feed Helen in the parked car, but Helen wasn't much trouble on the whole, and Mum was able to have a snooze while Rob, inspired by the match he'd watched the previous day, played one-stump cricket with Keith and did quite well at it.

On Friday morning, Keith took him to the zoo at the other side of town, and on Friday afternoon they went rowing on the park lake. Rob glanced across at the children's pool and saw that somebody else had replaced Mike. The island was definitely Pratt's Island today, and not the Paradise Island that Rob had visited so often. They rowed past it, but Rob didn't say anything to Keith. By Friday tea-time he was feeling more friendly towards Keith than he'd done before. But it was all spoiled when he went into the kitchen and found Keith and Mum embracing closely. That sent a stab of renewed hatred through him, and he rushed out of the room and wouldn't speak to them all evening.

And on Saturday morning he set off by bus to visit Dad at Crimley.

Part of the trip he spent looking out of the window, and part reading one of the battered adventure stories he'd brought from his shelf. He hadn't been to Crimley before, and he didn't think much of it. It was a Midland industrial town that had known better days, and a lot of the town centre was old and grimy.

Dad met him, and took him to a café for a meal. Conversation with Dad was never all that easy, but Rob had things to tell him about the week's excursions. Dad listened with interest, but by the time Rob got to

Thursday he realized that Dad was looking wistful. Dad was rather sad and silent for the rest of the meal.

In the afternoon they were going to the cinema, but first Dad took Rob to see his new bedsitting-room. Not that it was new at all. It was in a huge old house that had been converted into a number of flats and bedsitters. The ground and first floors had once been splendid and still had a kind of seedy elegance. You went up several flights of steps, which got narrower and shabbier all the way. Dad's room was right at the top, and Rob was shocked by it.

It was a former attic, and fairly large, but it was worse than shabby. It was crummy. There were damp patches on walls and ceiling, and a stained washbasin, and the furniture only looked fit for a junkshop. It didn't compare well at all with the neat, trim house where they'd all lived together.

Dad could see what Rob thought of it. He said apologetically, 'It was the best I could get, Rob. You should have seen some of the others I looked at, they were much worse. But what can I do? I can't *buy* a place on the wages I get, and there's nothing decent to rent.'

Rob said, 'You must be lonely, Dad.'

Dad said, 'Well, yes, I suppose I am, sometimes.'

'What do you do in the evenings?'

Dad said, 'Well, by the time I've got home and made myself a bit of supper and read the paper, there isn't all that much time to pass before bedtime. I have a radio, and like I said, I think I'll rent a telly.'

Rob said, 'Doesn't sound very exciting.'

'No, son, I suppose it isn't.'

'I mean, don't you have any friends?'

Dad said, 'Well, I'm beginning to get to know folk. But it takes time.'

Rob was silent. He wished he hadn't seen this depressing place, and he didn't like to think of the boring and lonely life Dad must lead. He was glad they were going out. Dad had remembered that he liked cherryade and had bought him a bottle of it. Good old Dad, he thought. Unlucky old Dad.

'Well, come on, son,' Dad said. 'The programme starts at half past three. If we don't go now, we'll miss the cartoon.'

They set off down the stairs. The last broad flight at the bottom ended in a spacious entrance hall. They were crossing its marble floor when the front door opened and a figure hurtled in. It was on a collision course with Rob. He sidestepped, not quite quickly enough. The figure tried to brake, began to slide on the slippery floor, lost its footing, grabbed at Rob, overbalanced, and threw Rob off balance too.

Rob sat down abruptly, with a painful bump. The incoming figure ricocheted from him, crashed into the nearest door, and came to rest in a sitting position opposite him. The figure was a girl of about Rob's age and size. She had tawny, unruly hair, and was wearing jeans and a tee-shirt. She sat, dazed and breathless, rubbing her shoulder. Rob got up, painfully, and rubbed his bottom.

'You all right?' Dad asked him.

'Yes.'

'And what about you, young lady?'

The girl grinned, wryly. 'I'm not dead yet,' she said.

'You want to watch where you're going, don't you?' said Dad. He was trying to sound severe, but Dad wasn't very good at sounding severe. The girl said 'Yes' and grinned again, and there was something about her grin that made Dad grin in response. 'You'll be more careful another time, I dare say,' he said.

Then the door she'd fallen against opened. A woman stood in the doorway. A woman who was obviously the girl's mother. She had the same tawny hair, though it was fading a little. Her face was round and slightly worn-looking, but pleasant enough. She was older than Mum. Mum had been very young when she had Rob.

'What goes on?' she inquired, and then, 'Katie! What are you doing down there?'

'Just admiring the view,' said Katie. She picked herself up.

'Oh, *you*!' said her mother.

Dad said, 'A minor accident, that's all. Nobody hurt.'

The woman said, 'I've told her before to watch out on that slippery floor.' And then, 'You're Mr I-don't-know-your-name from the top flat, aren't you?'

'That's right. Walter Little. This is my son, Rob.'

'I'm Rita Maguire. Katie's my daughter.'

Katie said, 'I just came for my anorak. Then I'm going back to Jane's.' She disappeared into the ground-floor flat, reappeared a few seconds later, and shot out of the building again.

'I bet she takes a bit of slowing up,' Dad said.

'She's always rushing around,' her mother agreed. 'Kids!' She and Dad stood looking at each other. There was an awkward pause. Mrs Maguire said, 'Well, we've met now, haven't we?'

'Yes,' said Dad. Another pause.

'And it looks like Katie and Ron have met,' Mrs Maguire said, smiling.

'Rob,' Dad corrected her.

'Well, we'll be seeing you and Rob around, I expect.'

Dad said, still looking awkward, 'Rob doesn't live with me, he's just visiting.' And then, hastily, 'We were going out to the pictures. The programme will have started.'

Mrs Maguire said, 'Oh, well, I mustn't keep you.' Dad and Rob went on their way. As they left the building, Rob said, 'Maybe she was going to ask you in for a cup of tea.'

Dad said, 'What makes you think that?' And then, without waiting for an answer, 'Do you know, she's the first person who's spoken to me since I came to this building.'

Rob remembered that on the way back to Selhurst. He felt so sorry for Dad, alone in that dreary place, that it actually seemed to hurt.

In the evening, Keith went to the pub, to play in a darts team. Helen was asleep, and Mum and Rob sat quietly together in the sitting-room. After a while Mum asked, 'Well, how was your dad, Rob?'

'Oh, all right.'

'What's his new flat like?'

'It's not very nice,' said Rob. He saw it in his mind's eye, dismal and unwelcoming. And with it came the memory of Dad's expression, so sad and hesitant. Dad had hardly been able to talk to Mrs Maguire. It was as if he expected all the time to be rebuffed.

'Dad's lonely,' said Rob; and suddenly he had to bite his lip to stop tears coming to his eyes. Then the words came out in a rush, 'Why did it have to happen? Why did you do it?'

He half expected Mum to fly at him, but she didn't. She was silent for quite a while. Then she said, 'I can't explain it all to you, Rob. There's parts you couldn't understand, not possibly. But it wasn't working out. It couldn't go on. It couldn't, Rob, honestly. If I *could* explain and you *could* understand, you'd see that it couldn't.'

Rob said, 'That doesn't tell me much.'

There were tears in Mum's eyes, too. She said, 'Come here, Rob.' She drew him to her and hugged him. 'I know you love your dad, Rob, and he loves you. And I love you too, I do truly. I'm sorry it has to be like this.'

'I don't know where I *am*,' said Rob. They were both weeping. Rob wouldn't have wanted Keith or the big boys or even Wayne to see him weep. But he felt better for it. He was tired after the day's journeying, went to bed early, and didn't hear Keith coming in. Or Helen crying.

Helen was teething. She cried again and again, all night long.

In the morning, Keith said, 'I'm sorry, Rob. We thought, when you were so upset, we might get by without you having to change your room after all. But it's no good, your mum isn't getting any sleep. Helen will just *have* to go into your room, and you to the back. I'll get on with clearing out the junk this morning. Are you

86

going to help me? You don't *have* to, but I'll be doing it anyway, whether you help or not.'

Rob had thought about it. If there was a fight over the room, it was a fight he wasn't going to win. He might as well save his ammunition for some more promising conflict.

'I'll help,' he said.

Keith beamed. 'Thanks a lot, Rob,' he said. 'I really appreciate that.' He took Rob's hand for a moment in his big, warm one. 'We'll make a good team when we settle down together, you and me.'

Rob couldn't help feeling pleased by Keith's approval, but he tried not to let his pleasure show. As soon as breakfast was over, they started work.

The back bedroom had never been slept in. When there'd only been Mum and Dad and Rob, it hadn't been needed. Gradually it had filled up with junk. Whenever there was anything they didn't need but didn't want to throw out, it went into the back room, so that they could close the door on it and forget it. The latest things to arrive had been property of Keith's from his former bachelor flat. The room was crammed to the doors.

Working through it was like going back in time. They found buckets and spades that had been bought year after year for Rob when he was small, to be taken on holiday. They found his discarded toys, too, including the battered old teddy-bear he'd once taken to bed with him every night. Keith said, 'I suppose we could keep that for Helen,' but Rob wasn't too keen, and on second thoughts Keith decided that a new baby was entitled to a new teddy-bear.

Keith was strong and a fast worker. He was also a ruthless thrower-out. Keith wasn't much interested in the past life of the house, and Rob didn't want to be reminded of it, so they didn't have any disputes over whether to get rid of things. By Sunday dinner-time the room was cleared and there was a small mountain of stuff outside on the front lawn.

Now it was empty, the room looked quite attractive. It had a dormer window and interesting slopes to the roof. It was bigger than it had looked when full of junk, and was more private than Rob's present room, being tucked away at the back of the house. Rob had to admit to himself that he rather liked it. If the change hadn't been forced on him, he wouldn't have minded at all. He couldn't help thinking how different it was from Dad's squalid bedsit.

'Not in bad condition, is it?' Keith said. 'After dinner I'll sweep it out and put a coat of emulsion on the walls. Then I'll borrow Jack Allen's van and run the junk round to the tip. That'll keep me out of mischief for a while.'

'Do you still want me to help?' Rob asked.

'Not unless you really want to,' said Keith. 'You've done a good morning's work. Why don't you go down to the lake and see your pal? Here's a pound for a boat, and another to spend in the park shop or the Pavilion, just as you like. I reckon you've earned it.'

Rob heard himself say, 'Thanks a lot, Keith.' Just for a moment they grinned at each other.

Going to the lake was exactly what Rob wanted. He hadn't told Keith or Mum that Mike had left. While ever they thought Mike was there, they'd be happy to let him go.

After dinner he walked down through the park, where there was no sign of Colin Baxter or Tim Weatherall, and made his way to the lake shore. The trip to Paradise Island was getting easier with practice. He didn't have to climb the beech tree. He sat down with his back to it and was there at once, without any effort.

He and Wayland were sitting at their home-made table in front of the log cabin, with Crusoe snoozing beside them and Billy Bones perched close by, making wise remarks. Between Rob and Wayland was the treasure map that the pirates had left behind.

Wayland said, 'I can't understand this map. And even if we find the treasure, we don't know who it rightfully belongs to.'

Rob said, 'I think *I* know.'

Out of the tangle stepped the castaway Dag, who had been gathering fruit. When his eyes fell on the map he was excited. 'That treasure is rightfully mine,' he said. 'It was my reward for bringing a ship with a hundred souls aboard safely round Cape Horn in stormy weather. I was robbed of it by pirates many years ago.'

The castaway added, 'I need that treasure. You see how thin and ragged I am. Without it I have nothing.'

Rob said to Wayland, 'I *knew* it was Dag's. His story has the ring of truth. We must help him to recover his treasure in his hour of need.'

Wayland said, 'Of course, Roberto. You are right as usual.'

Billy Bones squawked, 'Gold moidores! Doubloons! Pieces of eight!'

'But,' Wayland said, 'I still can't make head or tail of the map.'

The map was in faded black ink on yellow parchment, much creased. It only showed part of the island, and you couldn't tell which part. On it were a bit of land, a bit of sea, some trees, and a trail drawn in a dotted line. At the end of the trail was a cross, and beside it were the words HERE LYES YE TREASURE.

'That's all very well,' said Wayland, 'but it doesn't tell us where to start.'

'What about the writing underneath?' asked Rob.

'It's in code, Roberto,' said Wayland. 'I can't tell what it says.'

The message under the drawing read OG OT EHT TUOKOOL. TES A ESRUOC ROF REEHS DAEH. YTFIF SECAP TSAP DIPAR REVIR DNIF EGASSEM NO EERT.

'It looks double Dutch to me,' said Wayland. But Rob applied his keen intelligence to the puzzle.

'I have it!' he declared. 'It tells us to go to the Lookout, set a course for Sheer Head, and fifty paces past the Rapid River find a message on a tree.'

Wayland was full of admiration. 'I could never have decoded that,' he said. 'How did you do it, Roberto?'

'You wouldn't understand if I told you,' said Rob. 'Now, off we go. We must take a spade and axe.'

'Shall I come?' asked Dag.

'No, you wait at the cabin,' said Rob. 'I don't want you to come to any harm. This is a mission for strong young men.'

Rob led his little party on its way. Crusoe followed at his heels. Behind came Wayland. Billy Bones fluttered overhead, squawking 'Doubloons! Pieces of eight! Gold moidores!' They scaled the path to the Lookout, and from there set off across country in the direction of Sheer Head, with Krakatoa smoking gently on their left.

When they came to the Rapid River, they found it in full spate. But there were boulders strewn in the broad, furious torrent. Rob went first, leaping fearlessly from rock to rock. Wayland followed, and slipped into the raging waters, but Rob plunged after him and pulled him out.

Beyond the river, a path led into the Black Forest. A weird, screaming cry was heard, and the puma raced towards them between the trees, but when it saw Rob it instantly became tame and licked his hand before going off in search of other prey.

Counting out fifty paces, they came to a great tree, on whose trunk a skull had been crudely carved with a knife. Beneath the skull was cut a pair of bones, but they weren't crossed, they formed an arrow pointing away from the path in a westerly direction. And carved between the bones were the words NEEWTEB OWT SENOTS.

Once again, Wayland had no idea what this meant, but Rob could decode it. 'It says "between two stones",' he told the puzzled Wayland. 'We must go the way the bones point, and no doubt we shall come to the stones. The treasure will be buried between them.'

On went the little group, with Rob still striding boldly ahead. They came out of the forest into blazing sunshine and found themselves on the towering cliffs of Sheer Head, at the west end of the island. Set into the turf were many rocks, scattered as if by a giant hand.

'The treasure must lie between two of these,' said Rob, 'but which two?'

While Rob was considering the matter, Wayland carelessly disturbed a nest of deadly snakes. In a hissing, venomous bunch they attacked the party. Rob swung his axe back and forth, and head after head flew from body after body until all the snakes had been decapitated. But before the last snake could be killed, it had sunk its fangs into Wayland's ankle, and Wayland had swooned to the ground. Rob dropped to his knees, sucked at the punctures, and spat out the poison. Wayland began to recover, but was still feeble.

Suddenly Rob knew how to locate the treasure.

'Crusoe!' he called.

Crusoe bounded forward, wagging his tail.

'Sniff it out, boy!' Rob ordered him.

Crusoe sniffed around among the stones, and eventually started digging. Earth and stones flew. Rob took up the spade. With powerful movements he dug and dug until there was a great hole.

Nothing came to light, and Wayland would have given up, but Rob had faith in Crusoe and was not to be defeated. At long last, his spade chinked against something hard. Wayland had recovered enough to help him, and together they lifted a sea-chest from the hole. They raised the lid. The chest was full of rubies, diamonds, emeralds and golden guineas.

'This will be enough to make the poor castaway rich for life!' said Rob. 'He can buy a house of his own and have no need for crummy bedsits.'

With Wayland hobbling painfully at his side, Rob

made his way back to the cabin. The castaway, Dag, was waiting for them.

'Look!' said Rob. 'Here is all the wealth you could desire. I found it for you!'

The castaway was overwhelmed. 'You are truly a son to me!' he declared. 'No father could have a better one!'

But as Dag spoke Rob perceived the drawback.

'However,' he said, 'the treasure is of no use to you here. You cannot get it home. On the island it will buy you nothing. My efforts have been in vain.'

'Not in vain!' declared the castaway. 'You have shown me what great achievements you are capable of. And here on the island we are at least together. We will have happy times from now on, you and I and Wayland, to say nothing of Crusoe and Billy Bones. This will be Paradise Island indeed. It is your own place, Rob's place, and while you are here you are safe from everything.'

'And now we will feast!' said Wayland.

Rob realized that he was hungry. And with this realization, his mind floated away. He wasn't on the island any more; he was on the shore of Selhurst Park Lake, with his back to the beech tree; and he was stiff. He got up and went home to Sunday tea.

He arrived at the house to find a cheerful Keith waiting for him.

'Come and see what I've been doing while you were out!' Keith said. 'I just finished five minutes ago.'

He led the way to the back bedroom. In Rob's absence it had been transformed. Keith had put a coat of pale blue emulsion on the walls and a square of dark brown carpeting on the floor. He'd moved Rob's bed into the room, and also his wardrobe, his chest of drawers, his shelf of adventure stories and his radio-cassette player. And that wasn't all. Under the eaves, where there wasn't room to stand upright, Keith had placed a plastic-topped kitchen table, and on the table was a figure-of-eight racetrack with model cars.

'I knew you'd like that,' he said. 'Any lad would. Trains'd have been better, I admit, but there isn't room for a proper layout, and I don't think much of a piddling bit of railway on a table top.'

Rob stared at the racetrack. 'Where'd you get that?' he asked. 'It's Sunday.'

Keith winked. 'Got it off Jack Allen,' he said. 'I didn't ask any questions. It's brand new. Fell off the back of a truck, I reckon. And the table and carpet came from Solly Lightman's junk shop. Didn't cost me a penny. I called at Solly's back door, on my way to the tip, and traded a few of our throwouts with him. I've done a hard day's work for you, young Rob. I hope you're pleased.'

Rob was overwhelmed. For the moment he couldn't think what to say.

'I'll race cars with you later,' said Keith. 'We'd better go for tea now. Helen's asleep – touch wood – and I know your mum's made a good meal for us. We'd better not keep her waiting. In a minute she'll be saying it's all spoiled.' He grinned, and added, as one man to another, 'You know what women are!' Then, 'You haven't had much to say, Rob. Don't tell me you're *not* pleased!'

'It's great!' said Rob. And there was no denying that the room was much more attractive than he'd thought it could be. The car racetrack would be fun, too. Keith had taken a lot of trouble for him. But into his mind came a picture of Dad's squalid bedsit, and the contrast made him want to weep.

For a moment he felt an urge to shout out that nothing would change him from wanting his dad back here and everything as it used to be. But Keith was smiling at him, full of goodwill. He hadn't any wish to hurt or anger Keith – not just now, at any rate. There wasn't any way he could explain to Keith how he really felt.

8

Rob went to Paradise Island four times during the following week. They were good times. He and Dag and Wayland roamed the island together, fishing and swimming and gathering delicious fruit. Sometimes Rob took the lead and sometimes Dag, while Wayland was always the loyal supporter.

On his way down to the lakeside, Rob passed the glass-cased map of Selhurst Park, with the pointing arrow that said YOU ARE HERE. One morning, on inspiration, he took a sheet of flimsy paper with him, placed it over the glass, and traced on to it the outline of Pratt's Island. He spent contented hours in the next few evenings mapping Paradise Island on a large piece of cartridge paper, with the aid of a fibre-tipped pen and coloured pencils. He named the various features, from Cape Crossbones at the east end to Sheer Head at the west, and marked with crosses the spots where he'd rescued Wayland, discovered Dag, and found the treasure. Dotted lines indicated the routes he'd followed. It was all very satisfying. He didn't of course show the map to Mum or Keith; it was strictly private to himself.

Ordinary life was dull all week, with nothing much happening. The holidays were drawing to a close. Mum remarked that Rob seemed to be living in a world of his own, but as long as he didn't sulk or storm Mum didn't mind. What she needed most was peace.

And next time Dad came he was cheerful. He was liking his job. He'd rented a telly, which was working well. Mrs Maguire in the ground-floor flat had twice asked him in for a cup of tea, he said, and was a very nice lady.

Rob felt a pang of jealousy at this. He wasn't sure that he wanted any nice ladies in Dad's life. But Dad was so shy and quiet that Rob couldn't imagine him making advances to any lady, however nice.

That daughter of Mrs Maguire's, Katie, was a livewire, Dad went on. Did Rob remember how she'd cannoned into him? Rob remembered all right. He still had a bruise. But by and large it was good to see Dad looking cheerful, and quite a change.

Next day, Dean Hendrick came to the door for Rob. Dean lived a few doors up the street, and was a year older. He didn't usually bother with Rob. Rob soon found that Dean's friend Jeremy Fowler was away on holiday all week – the last before starting school again – and that he himself was only a second string. But he wasn't in a position to mind. Dean had plenty of pocket-money and wasn't mean with it. They had an interesting week, spending an afternoon in the amusement arcade in the town centre and another riding on the steam train that was operated as a hobby by the local rail preservation society.

When Dad telephoned on Friday to say he couldn't come on Saturday, Rob was only half disappointed, because he got an extra half-day with Dean. But on Sunday he had to pay the price for this temporary friendship. Jeremy had come home from his holidays,

97

Dean was no longer interested in Rob, and Rob felt more alone than ever.

On Monday morning, Rob was back at school. He'd moved up a class, and so had most of the children who'd been with him the previous year. His new teacher was Mrs Scott. In the past, Rob had always been well ahead with his work. But he didn't feel interested this year. When Mrs Scott asked him questions, he usually failed to answer because he hadn't been listening. She told him several times to pay attention.

He was missing Dad a lot by now, and looking forward to Saturday. So it was a blow when, half-way through Saturday morning, Dad telephoned to say that once again he wouldn't be coming this week.

'I didn't quite gather why,' Mum told Rob. 'Your dad doesn't always make things very clear. He's trying to get something fixed up that he reckons will benefit *you*, but I didn't really understand what it was.'

Rob had an uneasy feeling in his stomach. Last week he hadn't minded too much, but this week he minded a lot. Dad had missed three weeks in the last five. Rob thought once more about Sherry Canham, whose dad had stopped coming altogether. In bad moments Rob had always feared that this could happen to him. Today he'd have taken refuge on his island, but during breakfast the rain began falling, gently at first and then more heavily, from a dull grey sky.

'It looks to have set in for the day,' said Mum.

Rob knew it was no good suggesting that he should go down to the boats. Mum wouldn't have allowed it on a day like this. Anyway, he didn't feel at all sure he'd be able to transport himself to Paradise Island if he was soaked to the skin and sitting outside in the beech tree or on the lake shore. He mooched around the house all day, getting gradually more depressed, and spending a lot of time in front of the television without really watching it.

Keith, always optimistic, went with bat and flannels to the cricket field for the last match of the season. He came back at supper-time, still quite cheerful, having won three pounds at cards while sitting in the Pavilion waiting for the rain to stop. It hadn't stopped, and it didn't stop on Sunday either. Keith went out twice to play darts at the pub, but Mum and Rob sat glumly at home and Helen grizzled for a good deal of the time. Monday was fine, but Rob was back at school, where he sat silently and took as little part as possible in what was going on. Once Mrs Scott said, 'Robert Little, don't you ever take *any* notice of what I'm saying?' But Rob just allowed such remarks to flow over him.

On Tuesday, Mum told Rob, 'I've got a note from your teacher, Mrs Whatsername. She wants me to go and have a word with her about how you're getting on.'

'Does she?'

'What have you been up to, Rob? Have you been getting into trouble?'

'No.'

'There must be something.'

On Thursday, Rob came out of school to find Mum just arriving in the playground, pushing Helen in her pram.

'You just wait there, Rob,' she said. 'We'll all go home together.'

She went to find Mrs Scott, and was away for twenty minutes. Helen woke up and began to whimper. Rob leaned over the side of the pram and pulled faces. Helen seemed to like that, and grinned toothlessly at him; her teething hadn't yet produced visible results. Rob jogged the pram gently, and Helen still smiled. Mum came back and said, 'I'm glad to see you showing some interest in your little sister.' Rob said sullenly, 'I was only keeping her quiet.'

On the way home, Mum told him, 'Your teacher's worried about you.'

'Is she?'

'Unresponsive. That's what she says you are.'

'Does she?'

'She says you just sit there, not taking anything in. You're no trouble, she says, but she can't get through to you . . . Rob! Are you listening to me?'

'Yes.'

'She wondered if you needed help,' said Mum.

'Help to do what?'

'Professional help.'

'I don't know what you mean.'

'Well, somebody, a kind of doctor, to help you adjust. I had a good talk with Mrs Scott, and she understands how things are. We all know it's been a difficult time for you, and it *is* sometimes hard for children to get used to a new situation. But there are people who are, well, trained to help.'

'I don't want anybody helping *me*.'

'Well, *I* don't want to get involved with psychiatrists and such, any more than you do. I've enough on my plate without that. But you must try and be sensible, Rob, or we may have to do something. Keith and I are doing our best, and your dad too, and you must try to co-operate.'

'My dad hasn't been for two weeks now,' said Rob bitterly.

'I expect he has his reasons. He'll come this week, I dare say.'

By Saturday morning there was no word from Dad.

'That probably means he's coming as usual,' said Keith. But Rob was beginning to think that Dad's arrival was no longer usual. 'Maybe he'll never come again,' he said.

'Don't be silly,' said Mum. As she spoke, there was the ker-flop of the letter-box, and Mum went to the door. 'Well, maybe this'll cheer you up, Rob,' she said. 'A letter for *you*.'

Rob knew the writing at once. It was from Wayne. His face lit up.

'Great!' he said. 'I wondered if I'd ever hear from him.' He tore open the letter eagerly.

Dear Rob [it said],
Sorry for not writing sooner, it's kaos here, we are still only camping, there's a lot to do to the house, it's in a mess. There is a boy called Andy next door, he is all right, he has a computer and about a million games. Andy and his dad took me to the football, start of the season, their team is called United, they won 5–1, their striker is Graham Glossop, he scored a hat-trick. I think I will support United. Me and

Andy are making a den at the bottom of his garden, if you were here you could come in it but it is our den. Must stop now as I am going round to Andy's.
Your pal,
Wayne.

Jealousy boiled up in Rob. He and Wayne had been best friends for years, and now along came this Andy and it was all Andy. He shoved the letter in his pocket. There was no comfort in it.

'How *is* Wayne?' Mum inquired.

'Oh, all right.'

'Are they settling in at the new house?'

'Yes.'

'Is there any interesting news?'

'No.'

Mum didn't pursue the matter. Rob hung around all morning, hoping that Dad would ring, but he didn't. In the afternoon he went to the coach station at the usual time, and watched the people getting off the coach. There was no Dad. Rob waited a minute or two, then boarded the coach himself to make sure. No Dad.

He didn't stop to think what he was going to do. He ran from the coach station, and his feet took him to the park, down through the parking lot and on to the lake bank, where he flopped down breathless beneath the beech tree. He was on the island at once, without even trying. But the sky was grey instead of its usual vivid blue, and a thicker plume of smoke than before rose from Krakatoa. Today it felt more like Perilous than Paradise Island, and he was full of anxiety.

He hurried to the cabin where he, Dag and Wayland had made their headquarters together. But the cabin was empty. He had known it would be empty.

He stepped outside the cabin and called, 'Dag! Wayland! Dag! Wayland!'

There was no reply. He had known there would be no reply. He called again and again. Still no reply.

He climbed to the Lookout, calling all the way in vain. From the Lookout he surveyed the ocean, stretching endlessly grey in all directions.

Far out on the horizon was a sail. Rob knew what had happened. A ship had landed at the island and taken his companions off. They had deserted him.

But this was wrong. He was king of the island, the absolute ruler. Nothing could happen that he hadn't ordered. He wouldn't *allow* them to leave him in the lurch like that. He would bring the ship back to the island, disembark his repentant friends, and send the skipper on his way with a warning.

In his mind, Rob ordered the ship to return. But it didn't. The sail was sinking below the horizon. As he watched, it disappeared completely. There was only the ocean, bare and empty, and himself on the island, alone.

He didn't want to be there. And surely he didn't *have* to be there. He willed himself to leave the island and be back on the shore of Selhurst Park Lake. But that didn't work either. He willed himself harder and harder, and was still there in the Lookout. In the end he gave up and went slowly back downhill to the empty cabin.

Then he remembered his animal friends. *They* hadn't deserted him, surely. He called 'Crusoe! Crusoe!' and from somewhere in the Wilderness Crusoe came loping up to him, tail wagging, and leaped up in greeting.

'There, boy! *You* wouldn't let me down!' Rob said. Crusoe licked his face and Rob stroked Crusoe's head.

'Billy Bones!' Rob called. And with a welcoming squawk of 'Golden guineas! Gold moidores!' Billy Bones came flying up and perched on his shoulder.

Rob had friends after all. And the sky was clearing. Grey gave way to bright tropical blue. With Crusoe at his side and Billy Bones flying above and around his head and shouting to him, Rob set off to walk the island. Brilliant tropical birds sang, while trees flowered and fruited in riotous profusion. Rob didn't even try any more to bring his former friends back to the island. He was perfectly happy without them.

By the time he got back to the cabin, he was tired. He lay down on the couch he'd made for himself all that time ago, and fell asleep.

He woke on the lake bank, lying down. It must be tea-time now. He got up and set off home. At first he felt contented in the afterglow of his visit to the island, but gradually the everyday world took over, and along with it the misery of Dad's unexplained absence. By the time he got to the house, he was deeply depressed.

'Did your dad arrive?' Mum asked.

'No, he didn't!'

'Where have you been, then?'

'To the boats. Dad didn't ring?'

'No, he didn't. And you might have told me where you were going.' Then Mum added, concerned, 'I'm sorry, Rob. There'll be some explanation, I'm sure. I do wish your dad would get a telephone, though. It isn't nice, not to know what's happening.'

Keith had been playing football, for the first time in the new season. When he came in, half-way through the evening, Rob was staring blankly at the repeat on television of an episode from an ancient comedy series.

'You actually *watching* this crap, Rob?' he asked.

'Uh huh.' Rob didn't really know whether he was watching or not.

Keith said, 'I gather there's no word from your dad.'

'No.'

'Your mum thinks you're worrying about him.'

'Does she?'

'Don't worry, Rob. Like she said, there has to be a reason. But I'll tell you what. If we haven't heard from him by next week, I'll give the football a miss – there's reserves they'll be glad to try out in the team – and you and me'll go to your dad's place and see what's happened.'

Rob didn't say anything.

'You think that's a good idea, Rob?'

'What is?'

'You and me going over to make sure your dad's all right.'

'Don't see any point,' said Rob. He went on looking at the old comedy, though he didn't know or care what was happening on the screen. Keith pulled a face and went to get his supper out of the oven.

Next day, Keith was busy fitting cupboards in Helen's new room. In the afternoon, Rob escaped to the island again. He didn't make any attempt to bring Dag or

Wayland back. He didn't want any human being on the island. It was a place for himself and the animals. With Crusoe and Billy Bones he went in seach of the puma, which came instantly at Rob's whistle, played happily with Crusoe and didn't mind being teased by Billy Bones.

Rob trained the puma to sprint at words of command across the Great Plain, and Crusoe to do various tricks. He taught Billy Bones new words, too. They were all quick learners, thanks to his gifts as a trainer, and they loved every minute of it. They worshipped him. He basked in the warm sunlight and in the delight of their friendship. They were far nicer and much more fun than people.

When he got home, Mum asked him to join her and Keith in the sitting-room. The television was switched off. He knew from the way they were looking at him and at each other that they had something they wanted to tell him together.

Keith said, 'Rob, your dad rang this afternoon.'

Mum said, 'He'll be coming to Selhurst next week-end.'

Rob felt joy and relief. So his fears had been unfounded! Dad hadn't lost interest in him! Not that he'd really thought Dad would, but still, the fear had been real . . .

Keith added, 'He's coming to the house again.'

That wasn't quite what Rob wanted. He frowned.

'All right, Rob,' said Keith. 'I haven't forgotten what happened last time. But there's a special reason.'

'What's that?' Rob asked suspiciously.

Keith said, 'He's bringing . . . Oh, you tell him, Pam.'

'He's bringing a lady friend,' Mum said.

Rob was aghast.

'It's a Mrs Maguire,' said Keith. 'And her daughter. She's coming, too. Your dad says you've met them.'

'Yes, I've met them,' said Rob. 'That girl knocked me over. But my dad hardly knows them.'

'I guess he knows them better by now,' said Keith. 'He says Mrs Maguire's a really nice neighbour.'

'And it's just what he needs,' Mum said. 'To know somebody nice. I'll feel a lot better myself if I know he has a friend. Your dad's been lonely, Rob. You said so yourself.'

'But why should he bring her *here*? He comes to see *me*!'

'I suppose he wanted us to meet her,' said Mum uncertainly.

'Why? It's nothing to do with you.'

Mum winced.

Keith said, 'I suppose Walt must be serious about her, or he wouldn't be bringing her to Selhurst and introducing her to us.'

Mum frowned at Keith and said, 'I'm not going to discuss Rob's dad in front of him. Anyway, Rob, we've told you now. That's what's happening. You'll be seeing your dad on Saturday.'

Rob woke very early next morning, his heart thumping, and couldn't get to sleep again. A lady friend for Dad! He hated the thought. If Dad had a lady friend, that would mean he wouldn't bother to come. He'd missed three weeks in succession already. That was how it would be in future. Dad would be like Sherry's dad. Rob would lose him. And Dad was all he had in the world; well, almost all. It was the end.

Rob wept quietly in the darkness.

9

Ten minutes before the coach was due to arrive, Rob said, 'I'm going out now.'

Keith said firmly, 'Oh no, you're not.' And Rob knew he meant it. Keith had never laid a finger on him, but Keith was big and strong and speedy, and if he didn't mean Rob to get away, Rob wouldn't get away. It was no use trying. Rob waited with Keith and Mum.

Helen was outside in her pram. As soon as she'd fallen asleep, Mum had put her out in the garden and changed into smart clothes. It was months since Rob had seen her dressed up. She looked young and attractive.

Keith sat watching Saturday sport, his legs stretched out in front of him, at ease. Mum and Rob perched uneasily on the edges of chairs. Mum said, 'I hope we'll hear the doorbell, with the telly on. To say nothing of hearing Helen.'

Keith said cheerfully, 'You always hear Helen. It's old Mother Nature, isn't it? A mum can hear her baby in a thunderstorm.'

'You're the great expert on babies, of course!' said Mum.

She was smiling. Mum and Keith were always teasing each other. Mum and Dad had never been like that. Usually they were rather polite, but sometimes the politeness broke down, and then they'd come out with complaints against each other, complaints they'd been storing up for days or weeks or even months.

At that moment the doorbell rang loudly, as if to prove that it could be heard. Keith turned the sound down on the television, but didn't switch the set off. Mum went to the door. Rob stayed where he was. There were voices in the hall, and then they came into the room. Dad and Mrs Maguire and Katie.

Keith got up and stretched out a hand. As always, he was the biggest person in the room and seemed to take up the most space.

'Hello, there!' he said.

He was eyeing Mrs Maguire frankly. Keith looked frankly at everything and everyone. Mum inspected her, too, though not so obviously. Mrs Maguire was aware of being studied and seemed a little embarrassed. She was wearing make-up and looked younger than Rob had remembered, though still obviously older than Mum and not as smartly dressed. There were crows'-feet at the corners of her eyes. Her mouth was wide, and emphasized by the lipstick. Her expression was friendly enough.

Dad said, 'This is Rita. And this is her daughter, Katie.'

Rob wouldn't have recognized Katie. Instead of jeans, she was wearing a skirt and white knee-socks. You could see the resemblance to her mother in her face, which today had a well-scrubbed look. Her tawny hair was held down by a slide but looked as if it would spring back, given half a chance. She said politely, 'Hello.'

'Rob and Katie have met before,' Dad said. 'Collided,

you might say.' Then, awkwardly, to Mum and Keith, 'I thought it would be nice for you and Rita to meet. But we'll only stay a minute. We came to take Rob out, same as usual.'

Mum said, 'You've time for a cup of tea, though, haven't you?' She produced tea for herself and Rita and juice for Katie. Rob said he didn't want anything. Keith found two cans of lager for Dad and himself, and said, 'Well, Rob, you got a girl-friend today. Lucky lad, aren't you?'

Rob shrank into his chair, embarrassed. Katie looked wryly at him, and he thought she winked, but he wasn't sure. If she did, that made it worse. Keith went on, 'Why don't you two kids go into the garden? Be good.'

Mum added, 'Be quiet. Try not to wake Helen.'

Katie said, 'Okay,' and finished her juice. Rob didn't move at first, but Keith shooed the two of them out through the back door. As they went, Rob heard Keith, who never lowered his voice, saying, 'Well, now, it's great to meet your friends, Walt. Feel free to bring them, any time. Now, tell us how life's treating you.'

So! he thought. He was being pushed out. The grown-ups wanted to talk without him. Typical! Well, they needn't think he was going to be buddies with Katie. She was a stranger, and he would treat her as one.

Katie went straight to the pram and looked in at Helen.

'She's asleep!' she told Rob in a loud whisper.

Course she's asleep, thought Rob. If she was awake, she'd be howling. But he didn't say anything. Katie began gently rocking the pram. Rob was alarmed.

'Watch it!' he advised in a whisper. 'If you wake her up, there'll be trouble.'

'Mightn't she wake up anyway?'

'Maybe, but if she wakes up now it'll be our fault. I mean, *my* fault. Mum'll blame *me*.'

'All right.' Katie relinquished the pram. 'What shall we do?'

'What you like,' said Rob sullenly.

'It's a good-sized garden, isn't it? Wish we had one. We haven't any. Unless you count the window-box.'

Rob said nothing.

'That's a nice apple tree. They'll be ripe soon. What sort of apples are they?'

'Dunno.'

'I could just eat an apple now. There's lots of them. Would anybody mind?'

Rob said, 'It'd be sour. Anyway, there isn't one you can reach.'

'I could climb that tree. It looks easy. Is it?'

'I don't know,' said Rob. 'I've never tried.'

'You've never tried? I thought boys *always* climbed trees.'

'I don't have to if I don't want,' said Rob.

'Don't you like climbing?'

'Not specially.'

'Are you scared?'

'No. Course not. If I wanted to climb it I could.'

'Go on, then, do it.'

'You do it. It was your idea.'

'All right.' Then, in dismay, 'No, I can't. Not with my best clothes on. Mum'd be horrified.'

'Ha, ha, ha,' said Rob, slowly and derisively.

'I *could*, though.'

'Oh, yes, sure.'

'If I come again in old clothes, I *will*.'

Rob didn't like the sound of that. 'Who says you'll come again?'

'Well, you never know . . . What's in that shed?'

'It's only garden tools.'

'Can we go in it?'

'Not just now. The key's in the house.'

'You could *do* things with a shed like that . . . Have you any pets?'

'No.'

'Nor have I. We haven't room. I'd like to keep rabbits.'

'I wouldn't.'

'What would *you* like?'

'A dog.'

'So would I.'

'Dogs and rabbits don't mix.'

'I don't see why not. I wouldn't put the dog in the hutch . . . What sort of dog would you like?'

'Any kind.'

'I'd like an Old English sheepdog. If we had room for it. Or if we could only have a tiny dog, I'd have a Cavalier King Charles spaniel.'

Rob said nothing.

'Would you like a pony?'

'I don't know. I've never thought about it.'

'I would. But only if I had a big house. You can't keep a pony in a flat. I have a bike, though. I go out on it sometimes with Jane. But you can't cycle much in the middle of a town. I wish we lived in the country. Do you?'

'I don't mind.'

'Do you mind about *anything*?'

'Not much,' said Rob, and then, 'It's raining.'

So it was. In fact, quite suddenly, it was crashing down. They raced into the house.

The four adults had been talking, but the entry of Rob and Katie seemed to bring them to a halt. There was an awkward silence.

'Maybe it's time we were going,' said Dad.

'What, in *this*?' said Keith. And, to Rob, 'Why don't you and Kathy go to your room? You can show her your car racetrack.'

Rita said in an apologetic tone, 'Her name's Katie.'

Keith grinned and said, 'Sorry, Katie.' Katie grinned back and said, 'I'd like to see the racetrack.' Rob was afraid for a moment that Keith would jump up and get in on the act, but he only said, 'Go on, then, Rob. And remember what I told you. Behave yourself!' To his annoyance, Rob felt himself blushing.

Katie liked Rob's new room. 'Hey, this is good!' she said. 'I like the dormer and all the slopey bits. Wish I had a room like this!'

'I had a nicer one,' said Rob bitterly. 'It was taken away from me for the baby.'

'But this one's great . . . Hey, what's that?'

Rob realized with dismay that he'd left his map of the island out on the table, next to the racetrack. Katie was on to it at once.

114

'PARADISE (or PERILOUS) ISLAND,' she read. 'Sheer Head, Shipwreck Rocks, Quicksand Bay. It sounds like Treasure Island. Did you make it all up?'

'Give it me, it's mine,' said Rob.

'Oh, go on, let me have a look. The names are good, aren't they? I like Cape Crossbones. Did you get it from a book?'

'No, I didn't!' said Rob indignantly.

'You mean you made it all up yourself?'

'What if I did?'

'Well, it's clever, isn't it? Getting all this out of your imagination.'

Rob found himself feeling insulted at the suggestion that his island was imaginary.

'It's a real place,' he said.

'Go on!' Katie sounded impressed. 'Where?'

'It's in the park lake. Not far from here. But you can't get to it.'

'Why not?'

'They won't let boats land on it. But *I've* been there.'

It was good to have something to boast about. Rob went on, 'The man who hires out the boats – well, the one who used to – is a friend of mine. He's called Mike. He took me to the island, a few weeks ago. On a Sunday morning. Him and me, we gave it those names.'

'Wow! *I'd* like to go!'

'Well, you can't. Nobody can. But *I* might, if Mike comes back and does the job again.'

Katie looked at Rob with a mixture of respect and envy. Rob glowed. For the moment he was enjoying himself. That didn't often happen in real life; not these days. Katie took another look at the map and asked, 'What are the dotted lines? Are they trails? And the crosses?'

Rob became wary. He didn't want to give too much away. Paradise Island was his own place, and Katie was an intruder.

'I'm supposed to be showing you the racetrack,' he said.

He got it out and assembled it. They raced cars three times, and Rob won every time, which was satisfactory. Then Katie said, 'Look, the sun's come out. Shall we go in the garden again?'

'If you like. I don't mind.'

They went downstairs. Rita, sitting on the sofa, had relaxed a good deal and was telling a complicated story about an experience in the local supermarket. When Rob and Katie appeared, she interrupted herself.

'There, I do go on when I get going,' she said apologetically. 'Somebody should stop me. Isn't it time we were on our way, Walter?'

'Well, yes, love, I reckon it is,' said Dad.

Love! thought Rob. Yuk!

'Did you have fun with the car race?' Keith asked.

Katie beamed and said, 'Yes, thank you. Rob won.' Rob said modestly, 'I've played before.' Then he and Katie, Dad and Rita all went out for a walk. Rob didn't like the feel of that. They were walking out like a family, but they *weren't* a family. Dad wasn't Katie's dad and Rita wasn't his mum, and they shouldn't all be getting tangled up together.

The rain and the adult conversation had taken up quite

a lot of the afternoon. There was only time for tea at the Silver Tree café and a walk in the park before Dad and Rita and Katie had to go for the coach. At tea it struck Rob, and struck him like a blow, that Dad looked happier than he'd looked in months. Rob sulked all through the meal. But he couldn't put Katie off. When he got cross and sulky she stayed friendly, and that made him even crosser and sulkier. In the park, when he deliberately dropped behind, Katie dropped behind with him. She was cheerful as always, but not tactful.

'Your mum's new husband's hunky, isn't he?' she said.

'Uh huh.'

'Seems nice, too.'

'He's all right,' said Rob, trying reluctantly to be fair to Keith. Keith had done him no harm, except the single enormous harm of being there at all, and that was something he wasn't going to discuss with Katie.

'I suppose in a way you've got two dads.'

'No, I haven't. I've only got one. And I'll never have more than one!'

Katie was taken aback by his fierceness.

'Sorry-sorry-sorry,' she said. Then, 'I haven't got a dad at all.'

'What happened to him?' Rob asked. 'Did he walk out?'

It was Katie's turn to be fierce.

'No, he didn't!' she snapped.

'What did he do?'

'Died. That's what he did. Died. He didn't do it on purpose.'

Suddenly her face screwed up as if she was going to

cry. She turned away from Rob. He was perplexed and didn't know what to say. After a minute Katie turned back to him, giving her eyes a quick wipe with the back of her hand.

'Sorry,' she said again. 'It just came over me. I wasn't thinking about him, and then I *was*, if you know what I mean.'

'When did – when did it happen?'

'Two years ago. Took a long time. I don't often think about it now. But when I do it still hurts.'

Rob said, 'It hurts having your dad living away and somebody else living with your mum.'

'I suppose so. But at least your dad's *alive*. He's all right. I like him. Sort of gentle.'

'He's not hunky, though.'

'No. Shouldn't have said that, should I? Never mind. It's more important being nice than being hunky, isn't it? And your dad's nice.'

Katie was smiling again. Her distress had been as brief as a shower, and now the sun was shining. But she still wasn't tactful.

'My mum thinks so, too,' she said.

Rob said sourly, 'I suppose she must, to come all this way, and bring you as well.'

'She says he's the nicest person she's met since – since it happened.'

Rob remembered that Keith had supposed Dad must be 'serious' about Rita. Whatever that meant, Rob didn't like the sound of it. He didn't speak to Katie again the rest of the time they were together. And his resentment increased minute by minute. At the coach station, where they had a brief wait, Rita and Katie sat side by side on a bench while Dad took Rob's arm and guided him a little distance away.

'Sorry we've not had much time to talk,' Dad said. 'We'll make up for it later. I hope you've enjoyed yourself, anyway. It must have been a nice change for you, having young company.'

'I didn't enjoy myself at all,' Rob said. 'I hated it.' He broke from Dad's grip, and ran off without saying any goodbyes.

10

When Rob got home, Mum and Keith were in the sitting-room, both looking pleased.

'So that was your dad's lady friend,' said Keith cheerfully. 'She's all right, isn't she? And the girl's a livewire. I quite took to her. Didn't *you*, Rob?'

Rob didn't want to tell Keith how he felt. He sat down and reached for the television control.

Keith said, 'You can manage without the telly for a minute.'

Mum could read Rob's expression. She said, 'We both had a good talk with Rita. We think she's very nice, Rob. And you must try to understand. Your dad really does need somebody. It isn't much of a life for him on his own.'

Rob said, 'I don't care what he does. I'm going to bed. I'm tired.'

An hour later, when he was in bed but not asleep, Mum came to his room to say that Dad was on the phone. 'He wanted to be sure you were all right,' Mum said. 'And he'd like a word with you.'

'Tell him I've nothing to say,' said Rob. He turned over and closed his eyes. Mum went away. Rob opened his eyes again, and stared into the darkness. After another hour, Mum came back to find him still awake.

'Rob, love,' she said. 'Keith's gone to play darts. We can have a little talk together, just to ourselves, can't we?'

Rob said nothing. Mum went on, 'We really enjoyed meeting Rita and the little girl. Rita's had a hard life lately. It must have been a tragedy for her, losing her husband like that. And he was no age at all.'

Rob still said nothing.

'And with Katie to bring up, too. She's no older than you, Rob, though I think she *behaves* older, if you know what I mean.'

'She doesn't always,' said Rob, with memories of being cannoned into.

'I think they're *both* very nice. And, Rob, I do worry about your dad. I want him to be happy, you know. I do, really. You believe me, don't you, Rob?'

Her expression was earnest, almost pleading. Rob was tempted to say, 'It was you that made him un-happy.' But he couldn't do it. When Mum looked at him like that he wanted, in spite of everything, to put out his arms to her.

Torn both ways, he could only close down, set his face, and stay grimly silent. Mum sighed.

'It's all very difficult,' she said.

A thin wail came from along the passage.

'Helen's crying again,' said Rob, and escaped with relief from the conversation.

Next Saturday, Keith told Rob, 'Your dad rang. He's coming as usual this afternoon.'

'Is he?'

'I told him he could come to the house any time he liked and he'd be welcome. But he thought it was best for you to meet him at the bus station as usual. I suppose he's right, really.' A pause. 'Don't you *ever* have anything to say, Rob?'

'What *is* there to say?'

Rob saw the bus come in, but didn't jump up and go to meet it. He sat slumped on a bench, looked the other way, and pretended not to notice until Dad said, 'Hello, there.' Then he said, 'Hello,' without a smile, and stared at his shoes.

'Not so warm, is it?' said Dad. 'The weather, I mean.'

'I hadn't noticed.'

'Getting to be really autumn.'

'Is it?'

'I thought we might go straight to the pictures. Quite a good film at the Regal, from the sound of it.'

Rob said nothing, but allowed himself to be taken to the cinema, where he refused an ice-cream and sat in silence all through the film.

'Well, did you like it?' Dad asked when they came out.

'It was all right.'

The Silver Tree wasn't crowded, and they got a corner table with nobody within earshot. Dad said, 'Aren't you speaking to me today?' Rob just looked at him.

Dad said, 'What's the matter, son? Are you cross because I brought Mrs Maguire last week?'

No reply.

'She's been a good friend to me, Rob, since I moved into my new place. And I've got quite fond of Katie.'

'But why did you have to bring them here?'

'Well . . . I thought it would be nice for Rita to see Selhurst.'

'Didn't take you long to start calling her Rita, did it?'

'It's her name. I can call her by it, can't I?'

'Oh, sure!' said Rob; and then, 'What's special about Selhurst? It's just a place.'

'The park's pretty good. I thought it would make a day out for Katie. And I thought Katie might cheer you up a bit. You seem in the doldrums these days. I expect you could do with somebody young and lively around.'

'And maybe I couldn't.'

'Didn't you like Katie?'

'Not much.'

Rob realized as he spoke that this wasn't quite true. Most of the time Katie had been at his house he'd liked her well enough. It was just that he didn't want other people coming between him and his dad.

Dad sighed. Then he said, 'Actually, Rob, I have news for you. I'm hoping to get a job in Selhurst at last. Heaven knows I've been trying long enough. It's not certain, but there's a good chance.'

For a moment Rob was overjoyed. Dad back in Selhurst! That would be terrific. But the joy hardly lasted at all before it was overtaken by suspicion.

'Is *that* why you brought them here?' he asked.

'Well . . . I suppose it's another reason.'

'What are you *doing*, Dad?' Rob's voice was agonized. 'Are you going to *marry* Mrs Maguire or something?'

Dad said, 'Don't jump to conclusions. Nobody's said a word about any such thing.'

'You didn't say "No!"' Rob accused him.

It was Dad's turn to be silent. Rob went on, bitterly, 'You used to come *every* week, and it was just you and

123

me. And now you keep missing. And when you do come, you bring a woman!'

'I won't have you talk like that. She's not a woman; she's a real, nice lady, and I'm glad to have her as a friend.'

Rob said, '*I* haven't anybody, except you. Mum's busy with Helen all the time. And Wayne went, and Mike went, and I don't like any of them at school, and I haven't even a pet!'

Dad said, 'I'm sorry about that, Rob. But I can't be *everything* to you, can I? And, like I say, I thought it might be nice for you to meet new friends.'

Rob said, 'Well, it wasn't!' He felt an impulse to hurt Dad, and gave way to it. 'I want to go home,' he said. 'I mean, I want to go back to Mum and Keith.'

'There's half an hour before the bus leaves.'

'I know.'

Dad said, putting a brave face on it, 'Well, it's good that you should want to be with your mum.'

'Oh, it's not that,' Rob said.

'What is it, then?'

'There's something I want to watch on telly.'

It seemed to Rob that Dad looked suddenly small, crumpled and defeated. And it gave him a savage, horrible pleasure. It served Dad right for bringing other people along.

'I'll go home by myself,' he said. 'Don't worry, I won't run away.' He got up and walked towards the exit.

'Rob!' came Dad's voice in an appealing tone from behind him. But he took no notice and stalked out, and Dad didn't pursue him into the street.

For half a minute, Rob felt satisfaction with the hurt he'd inflicted. The satisfaction was succeeded by sheer, deep misery. He trudged home. Keith had gone round to the pub and Mum was bathing Helen. He switched on the television and sat in front of it all evening without changing channels.

Most of the time he was asleep with his eyes open and the images on the screen making no impression. And when he went to bed he didn't feel sleepy at all. He lay awake thinking of Dad, of the possibility that Dad would remarry and not have time for him any more. Maybe Rita, like Mum, would have a baby. She was probably young enough. Rob felt infinitely alone.

And then, without warning, he was on the island. He hadn't had to go to the lake bank, he hadn't tried or wanted to be on the island. For the first time, it had just happened. He was on Welcome Beach. And the sky was grey, the sea was grey, there was an air of dampness and mist. Everything was strange. It felt as if it had been a long time since he was here before.

Rob walked round to the landing-stage and the cabin. The cabin was empty, the door hanging loose and open. A creeper had thrust its tendrils through the windows.

Rob called, 'Crusoe! Crusoe!' There was no reply. He called 'Billy Bones!' but no Billy Bones came fluttering and squawking towards him. He picked up a stick and set out to walk his domain, calling and calling for Billy Bones and Crusoe, but without any result. Silence was all around him, as grey as the mist. The usual birdsong of the island was absent. Everything was damp, and he could only see a few yards ahead along the path. But he plodded on. He had to go on.

The path took him across the island to where the Rapid River ran out into Quicksand Bay. Here he was halted. The Hanging Bridge was down, its loose ends dangling into the torrent. Rob followed the river-bank down on to the sand, where the river became broad and shallow and he could wade across. He felt his footsteps sinking into the sand. He pulled out his heavy feet, took a step or two, and began to sink again. Dragging his feet from the sand with enormous effort, he trod through the stream and laboured onward at the other side. At each step the sand sucked at him. But he was off the beach at last, and finding the path again he pushed on through the Black Forest.

This was the territory of the puma. He whistled for it, but it didn't come. He whistled and whistled before walking on. Then he saw it, stretched along a branch of a tree ahead of him. It was snarling. He whistled, and the puma snarled again. Then it leaped at him, all friendliness forgotten. Rob dodged. The puma flashed past and turned towards him. He extended a hand and asked the puma, 'Have you turned against me? Why?' But the puma merely snarled, then launched itself at him again.

Rob defended himself with his stick. The puma clawed and bit. Rob fought. He didn't want to kill the puma, but if he didn't the puma would kill him. Finally he struck it a huge blow on the side of the head, and it fell motionless. Rob grieved for the puma, for it had been his friend.

Then he pushed on. At Sheer Head he came out on the

cliff top. Below him was the entrance to Skull Cave, where he'd found the castaway Dag. Now that Dag had deserted him, the cave was empty. Smoke rose sulkily from the summit of Krakatoa. Rob skirted its lower slopes and headed eastward across the Great Plain. And now he knew where he had to go. Ahead of him rose the hill on top of which was the Lookout. That was his destination.

The hill was steep, steeper than he'd remembered, and as he pressed on it grew steeper still. Eventually he was taking only one step at a time, with long rests between steps. As he rose, he could see more and more of the island, and the ocean disappearing into the mist all round it. The mist was thinning now, but everything remained desolate. Rob pushed on, step by painful step, until at last he was at the top, where the round temple with its stone columns stood.

He knew now what it was. It wasn't a temple to some mysterious unknown god. It wasn't a temple at all, though it was a refuge, a sanctuary. It was his, and it was his alone. The island surrounding him was alone in the sea that in turn surrounded it. And there was no life on the island, no life in the sea. There was nothing anywhere but himself. He was alone in a temple of aloneness, and it was where he would stay.

Thought drained out of him, and so did feeling. He didn't care any more about Crusoe or Billy Bones or the puma. He didn't care about anything or anybody. All he could see was the grey of sea and sky, grey within grey, grey beyond grey, nothing anywhere but grey. But he had quiet, and he hadn't any worries, any anxieties. Here in the temple he was through with everything; he was safe, and nothing could touch him. He could stay in the temple for hours, days, weeks, years, centuries. He didn't ever want to leave it again.

Rob lost count of time, but to some corner of his mind came the awareness that he was cold, that cold was spreading through him. With the awareness of cold came panic. If he stayed he would be chilled to death. He had to escape. He tried to walk out of the temple, but the temple itself resisted him. Between each of its ring of pillars was an invisible barrier that he couldn't cross.

He threw himself from one opening to another and still couldn't get out, but his action had an effect, for the temple began to dissolve around him. Like someone who knows he's been dreaming, Rob knew he was outside the temple, was away from the island and on the way back to the world of his troubles, and of his life. He was lying pyjama-clad on his bed, his window open to the autumn night air and his duvet lying on the floor. He picked it up, snuggled into it, and went to sleep.

On Monday evening, Keith called to Rob that Dad was on the phone. Rob said he didn't want to speak to Dad. On Tuesday Dad phoned again, and Rob still wouldn't speak to him. On Wednesday evening it was Mum who answered the telephone. She rested the receiver on the hall table, came to Rob, and said quietly, 'Rob Little, you are going to speak to your father. You understand? Go – to – that – telephone.' There was a note in Mum's voice that Rob had heard from time to time over the years and that he recognized. It was the note of final authority. He went to the phone.

'Rob! That you?' Dad asked.

'Yes. What do you want?'

'Rob! Oh, it's good to hear your voice. I've been worrying about you since Saturday. Are you all right, Rob?'

'Of course I'm all right. Why shouldn't I be?'

'You seemed so miserable on Saturday, I wondered afterwards if you were sickening for something. Your mum says you're well, but ... Seems *she* can't get through to you, either.'

Rob didn't say anything. In the silence, pips went for Dad to put more money in the box. Then he said, 'Rob – son – I want you to be happy. That's what matters most to me in the world.'

Rob said, coldly, 'Is it?'

Dad said, 'And if it came to the point, I wouldn't do anything to make you *un*happy. You understand?'

Rob didn't understand at first. It just sounded like words, not meaning anything. People kept on talking about other people's happiness, but nobody gave *him* any happiness. Then it came home to him what Dad was saying.

'You mean,' he said, surprised, 'you wouldn't marry that woman if I didn't want you to?'

Dad said, 'Oh, Rob, I wish you wouldn't think of her like that. But yes, it *is* what I mean. I wouldn't marry anybody if you really hated it. So you see, you've nothing to worry about. If the day came when you didn't mind, and if she was willing, then I suppose I might – I suppose she might – well, I suppose it might happen. But I'm not going to spring anything on you.'

Rob was silent once more, digesting this. Dad went on, 'You see, Rob, I put you first and I always will. Now, could I have a word with your mum before I run out of change?'

Rob brought Mum to the phone. He heard her ask Dad for the number of the box, so she could call him back. Then she sent Rob out of the way before doing so. She was on the phone to Dad for quite some time. Meanwhile Rob pondered. Shouldn't he be overjoyed? Dad wasn't going to desert him in favour of Rita, or presumably of anybody else. Rob still came first. Dad had said so. He, Rob, was Number One. Yet somehow he didn't actually feel cheered.

Mum joined him eventually. 'Well, Rob,' she said, 'your dad's just told me what he told you.'

'Has he?'

'You want to know what I think about it, Rob?'

Silence.

'I think your dad's out of his tiny mind, I do really. I told him so. "It isn't in *anybody's* interest," I told him, "to give the lad a veto on what you do. You've a perfect right to remarry if you want," I said, "and Rob can like it or lump it, and if it's somebody as nice as Rita he'll get to like it." That's what I said. But you know your dad, he can't bear to upset anybody, least of all *you*, and he says anyway he hasn't asked Rita and quite likely she wouldn't have him, and so on. And I'm telling you all this, Rob Little, because I think it's high time you got a grip on yourself and behaved like a sensible person. You're old enough now.'

Rob said, 'There's a programme I want to watch. It starts in two minutes.'

Mum drew in breath, exasperated. 'Oh, I give up!' she said. 'Of all the problems we have, I do believe you're the worst! Maybe you *should* see a psychiatrist. Though I can't believe he'd get anything out of you. I don't believe *anybody* could!'

Rob switched on the television. Mum didn't say any more. But he knew she was thinking about him all evening. She gave him troubled looks from time to time, and Rob knew that when he'd gone to bed and Keith had come in they'd be talking about him. He didn't care.

At school, he went through the week in the usual daze. He behaved himself, spoke when he was spoken to, answered questions when they were put to him, but showed no interest in anything or anybody. He'd been worried when term began in case Colin Baxter and Tim Weatherall were still after him, but it was obvious that they weren't. They had taken to following the big girls around, a few paces behind, making remarks and sniggering. They weren't interested any more in bullying smaller boys.

Rob hadn't any wish to go to Paradise Island now. His friends had departed from it, he didn't seem to control events there any more, and it was no longer a refuge. He was beginning to feel afraid of it. The alternative name of Perilous Island suited it better, and he would keep away.

But on Thursday night he went there anyway, and

once again it was without intending to do so. As soon as he got to bed, he felt it coming over him. The bedroom around him was dissolving. He was in mid-air, in no time and no place, and in a moment his surroundings were going to resolve themselves into the island where he no longer wished to be. He struggled against the transition. It was like a struggle against going to sleep, and perhaps it *was* a struggle against going to sleep, for clearly he was on the frontiers of dream.

Rob jerked himself awake and tried to think of other things. All he could think of was Dad in the crummy bedsit and Rita and Katie in the ground-floor flat below, and he could feel the pull of attraction between them as if it was in himself. Mum had always said he was like his dad, and he knew in his bones that it was so, for better or worse. Dad wasn't much good at putting things into words, but he could feel for Dad and Dad could feel for him, and that was why they were so involved with each other.

He turned the situation over and over in his mind, until he felt himself drifting away again; and again he knew that from drifting he would land on the island, and again he didn't want to do that. He heard Mum and Keith come upstairs to bed. Mum was trying to get Helen off her late-night feed, and Helen wasn't always co-operative, but tonight there was no sound from her.

Rob kept himself awake by listening out. When the house was silent, he put his bedroom light on, intending to read. His eye ran along his bookshelf. When it fell on *Treasure Island*, *The Coral Island* and other island stories, he looked away; he didn't want to read anything about islands. In the end he chose a science-fiction novel. But it didn't grip him. His concentration began to fail and his mind to wander again.

He got out of bed and went to the bathroom for a drink of water. Then he felt, or imagined he felt, hungry. He tiptoed downstairs and went to the fridge. There was an opened pack of sliced ham. Rob extracted a slice, and was making himself a sandwich when Helen began to cry.

Rob stayed where he was. She might go off again, he thought. But she didn't. The cries grew louder and more insistent. Rob switched off the kitchen light, crept to the foot of the stairs, and waited for Mum to go to Helen's room. Once she was safely inside it and feeding Helen, he could sneak past and go to his own room. And a minute later he heard the padding of Mum's slippered feet and the swish-swish of her dressing-gown as she went from her bedroom to Helen's. He climbed the stairs on tiptoe, and was just passing Helen's door when it opened and Mum came out again, almost bumping into him. She blinked, and her eyes fell on the bread and ham that were still in his hand.

'You've been raiding the fridge!' she said.

'Yes. I was hungry. I didn't want to wake anybody up.'

'Heaven help us, child!' said Mum. 'Don't I feed you enough?'

Then the crying began again. 'Oh, *no*!' said Mum. 'I might have known it was too good to be true. I'll have to feed her. Eat that up and go to bed, Rob Little. I'll talk to you in the morning.'

Rob found he didn't want the sandwich after all. He put it down the lavatory. Then he went back to bed. And further resistance was useless. Within a minute he was drifting away again, and the island was materializing around him, the island that by now was hateful.

He was outside his cabin. No Crusoe, no Billy Bones, no birdsong. He was alone, and he knew where he had to go. Up to the Lookout, to the circular stone temple or whatever it was. He was reluctant, but his feet would take him there.

He looked the other way, across to Krakatoa. Smoke was rising from it. One day Krakatoa would erupt, but there was no telling when. Then, as he watched, a figure came into view. It was making its way slowly and uncertainly across the Great Plain towards him, from the direction of Sick Man's Swamp. It was the former castaway, Dag.

Rob went to meet Dag and clasped him in his arms. 'What happened?' he asked.

Dag said, 'I came back. I could not abandon you. I had landed elsewhere and found companions, but I have returned to you of my own free will.'

Rob said, 'Then we are together again on the island and will never part.' But he saw that Dag looked sad and ill.

'What is wrong, Dag?' he asked.

Dag said, 'The island is not a good place, not any more. Nothing lives here. And I do not trust that volcano. We must leave before disaster strikes, as I fear it will!'

Rob said, 'The ocean is wide, and we could be lost or drowned.'

Dag said, 'My boat is small, but it is sound and sturdy, and will carry us safely for as long as is required. It is lodged in Sick Man's Swamp. By the time I reached the island I was exhausted and had not the strength to bring it round to the Anchorage.'

Rob said, 'You need time to recover. My cabin is in poor repair, so I will take you to Skull Cave, where you lived before, and make you comfortable.'

With Rob's arm round Dag's shoulders, they staggered across the plain and round the lower slopes of Krakatoa. Rob helped the feeble Dag to scramble down to the cave. Dag's old bed was still in its place inside, and Rob put the sick man to bed.

'You must rest until you are well,' he said. 'I will go and fetch food for us.'

Rob left the cave. He went first to his cabin, and found his axe. From the cabin he went to Sick Man's Swamp, where Dag's boat lay, as Dag had said, drawn up on the marshy shore. For Rob was afraid to leave the island or to leave Dag any means of abandoning him again. He took up the axe and crashed it into the timbers of the little craft. As he did so he felt guilt, terrible guilt; but he couldn't stop himself. Again and again he swung the axe, breaking up Dag's vessel, preventing any escape.

Then, suddenly, everything vanished, and he was in bed with the light on, and Mum, in dressing-gown again, was shaking him into wakefulness.

'What*ever* goes on, Rob?' she demanded. 'You were thrashing around in bed and punching your pillow!'

'I didn't want to!' cried Rob in distress. 'I didn't want

135

to break up his boat! I didn't, I didn't, it was happening in spite of me!'

And then he was fully awake. He said, 'I had a bad dream, Mum, that was all.'

'I'm not surprised,' said Mum, 'if you *will* eat ham sandwiches in the middle of the night. It serves you right. And do you know, I've been up twice tonight already?' She shook her head, wearily; then, surprisingly, she stooped and kissed Rob on the forehead. 'You're all flushed,' she said. 'I hope you're all right.'

'I *am* all right.'

'Go to sleep, then,' Mum said.

Rob did, and slept without any dream that he could remember until it was time to get up and go to school.

Mum didn't in fact say anything to Rob next morning about his raid on the fridge or his attack on his pillow, though she looked at him from time to time all through breakfast with a thoughtful expression. He got home from school that afternoon to find that Helen was asleep and Mum was speaking to someone on the telephone. Rob switched on the television and plonked himself on the sofa in front of it, letting the programme hold his eyes but not paying any attention to it.

The telephone conversation went on for some time. It was still in progress when a commercial break came and Rob went to the bathroom. On the way back he over-heard the word 'Rita'. It startled him out of his coma. He switched off the television, and when, a minute or two later, Mum hung up and came into the sitting-room, he was waiting for her. He faced her accusingly.

'I heard you say "Rita".'

'Yes.'

'That's Mrs Maguire, isn't it?'

'Yes.'

'Was it her you were talking to?'

'Yes.'

'Why?'

'I don't have to explain myself to you, Rob. But I'll tell you gladly why I was talking to Mrs Maguire. I was making an arrangement with her. I've invited Katie to come for this weekend.'

'You've *what*?'

'You heard, Rob. I've invited Katie, and she's coming on Saturday morning. And Monday's her half-term holiday, so she can stay till Monday evening if she likes.'

'But *why* did you ask her?'

'Because I wanted to, that's why.'

'You didn't say anything to me about it.'

'You've been so difficult lately, Rob, there didn't seem much point. But Keith and I both liked Katie, and it seems she liked Selhurst. And you really do need young company, Rob, you're getting so wrapped up in yourself.'

'And what about Dad?'

'He won't be coming this weekend. We all decided it was for the best, considering how things have been lately.'

'I don't want everybody deciding things for me. And I don't want Katie.'

'All right, Rob, so you don't want her. That's just too bad, isn't it? She's coming anyway, because *we* want her, and you can like it or lump it.'

'I *hate* Katie. And Rita. And you. I hate everybody.'

Mum was very cool.

'All right, Rob,' she said. 'You needn't shout. I heard you. You hate us all. I'm afraid that will only hurt *you*, Rob. We all have our lives to live, whatever you think about them.'

'I won't have anything to do with that girl, anyway.'

'Please yourself, Rob. I'm looking forward to having her here. We shall do our best to give her a good time.'

'You won't get any help from me,' said Rob. And he wasn't with Mum and Keith when Saturday morning came and they walked down, with Helen in her pram, to meet Katie's coach at the bus station. He'd slipped out early and gone to the park. There was an autumn nip in the air. Leaves, all shades of yellow and brown, had snowed on to the grass, and the boats had closed down for the winter.

Rob kept well away from the lakeside. He still hadn't any wish to go to his island. He was a little scared in fact of finding himself there once more at a time when he hadn't intended it.

He got back to find Mum in the kitchen. For a moment there was an expression on her face that told him she was relieved to see him. But she didn't admit it, and she didn't reprove him for not being there when Katie arrived.

'Well, well,' she said. 'The return of the wanderer! Welcome home!'

Rob, as usual, said nothing. He went into the sitting-room and reached for the control of the television set. Mum followed him through and stopped him.

'Just in case you're interested,' she said, 'Katie's here.'

Rob remained silent. Mum went on, 'And we're going to enjoy having her. That child really is *fun* to have around.'

'Not like me, eh?' said Rob, knowing perfectly well what Mum was thinking.

'Well, you said it, I didn't. But since you *have* said it . . . Oh, Rob, why can't you be like that? You were so nice when you were younger. So bright and helpful and responsive. Nobody would think now that you're the same boy.'

'Something must have happened to me,' said Rob bitterly.

'Something happened to *her*, poor mite. Her father dying under her own roof. But she's pulled out of it. She's a real trouper. She changed Helen's nappy for me, and she helped me make a pie . . .'

'And you wish *I'd* change Helen and make pies.'

'Oh, I don't mind about that, though it *is* nice to have a bit of help. But if you'd just behave like a human being among other human beings, that would do for me . . . Don't you want to know where Katie is now?'

'Not particularly.'

'I'll tell you anyway. She's up in Helen's room, helping Keith build a cupboard.'

'*My* room that used to be,' said Rob.

'Well, *that's* nothing to do with Katie. Why don't you go up there and see how they're getting on?'

'Why should I?'

Mum said, 'Rob, *please*, try and make things a little easier for everyone. Go and be civil to Katie. She hasn't done you any harm.'

Rob glowered. Then he said, 'Oh, all *right*,' and went upstairs.

Keith and Katie weren't in Helen's room, building the cupboard. They'd given themselves a break, and were in *his* room, racing cars against each other. He was furious.

'That racetrack's *mine!*' he said. He knew he was being mean and childish, and he didn't like it, but he couldn't prevent himself.

'Oh, come off it, Rob!' said Keith. 'You don't grudge Katie a game, do you?'

In the silence that followed, Katie said, 'Hello, Rob.'

Rob didn't respond to that. He said, 'Seems as if *nothing's* mine in this house. People coming into my room, using my things . . . I'm fed up!'

Another time, Keith might have exploded. More than once in the last few weeks, Rob had felt himself close to getting walloped. But Keith was keeping himself under control. He said patiently, 'Sorry, Rob. I didn't think you'd mind. If you'd been here, I expect you'd have played with Katie yourself.' And then Keith went on, 'Hey, Rob, I like your map!'

Rob was infuriated even more. The map was more private than anything else. It was bad enough Katie having seen it when she was here before, but for *Keith* to have seen it was worse still.

Katie said swiftly, 'You'd left it lying out again, Rob.'

'I didn't expect people to come barging in!' said Rob.

Keith ignored this and said brightly, 'I knew at once what it was a map of. Pratt's Island. I recognized the shape. Made a map of it myself when I was a lad, years ago. But I never thought of putting all those fancy names on it. Hadn't the imagination, I guess.'

Rob said, 'Give it to me!' and held out his hand.

Keith handed it over. 'I went there, too,' he said. 'Me and some other lads.' He was grinning at the recollection. 'We made ourselves a raft and paddled it out. And we couldn't even swim. They didn't teach you to swim at school in those days. It's a wonder we weren't all drowned. We had a bit of fun on that island. And we found an old round summer-house or something, and all carved our initials on it. I remember that.'

Rob recalled the carved initials, and in spite of himself he was interested. 'We saw those,' he said, 'Mike and me, when we went there. The first set of initials was K. H. That must have been you.'

'That's right,' said Keith with satisfaction. 'I was always first. I was the boss in our gang.'

'We pretended it showed savages had been there,' Rob said. 'Like Man Friday's footprint.'

'Yes, well, savages is about right,' said Keith. 'Young savages is what we were. The park-keepers all knew us. We were always up to some mischief or other. They chased us again and again, and sometimes they caught us. There was one of them – Olly Atkins was his name, he must have retired long ago – who could run faster than any of us. And if he caught you, you got a clip over the earhole. They didn't think of having you up in the Juvenile Court in those days.'

Keith was still grinning reminiscently. Then he said suddenly, 'Hey, kids! We could still have a bit of fun! How about it? Are you game?'

Rob stared.

Keith said, 'I've got a great idea for an adventure. Listen to this. Trev Norris – he's one of my pals at the Middleshire Arms – has an inflatable dinghy. Why don't I borrow it from him tomorrow morning, take it in Jack Allen's van to the far side of the lake, and row you two to the island? Nobody'll see us if we're careful. You can both carve your initials alongside those that me and my pals carved all those years ago. How about it?'

Looking at Keith, Rob could see exactly what he'd been like as a small boy. A cheeky, devilish expression. Come to think of it, Keith was still a great big small boy at heart.

But his latest idea made Rob feel weak in the legs. Rob's imaginary island had come to feel threatening to him. He didn't know why, but he suddenly felt sure that to set foot on the real-life island while in thrall to the imaginary one would be dangerous.

'There's a ten-pound fine for landing,' he said.

'So what?' said Keith. 'No more than a parking fine, is it? In fact it *is* a parking fine, sort of.' He laughed, pleased with the comparison. 'Anyway, they've got to catch you first, and we're not going to be caught. It'll be like old times. You can be my gang, eh?'

Rob hesitated. He still hated the thought.

'Come on, Rob! Don't be a wimp!' Keith urged him.

And the fear of Keith's contempt triumphed over Rob's fear of the island. He heard himself, to his own surprise, saying casually, 'Sure, Keith, I'll come.'

'Good lad!' said Keith heartily. 'And *you'll* come, Katie, won't you? You're not the kind to hang back from an adventure, *I* know!'

Katie had been looking doubtful, but now she said steadily, 'If Rob's going, I'll go.'

'That's great!' said Keith. 'Now remember, Rob, not a word to your mum. There's no need for her to know anything about it. I'll think up a cover story. This is *our* expedition, eh, gang?'

12

Rob woke on Sunday morning with butterflies in his stomach and a sense of threat and panic. He didn't feel safe in bed. His island – Paradise Island – was close to him. He was being drawn towards it, and he didn't want to go.

He got up and went to the bedroom window. It was a misty grey autumn day. He sat on the window-seat, looking out. In the garden of the house that backed on to his, a man and his son were raking up fallen leaves and twigs. Rob watched them intently, trying hard to keep his grip on the everyday world.

But he couldn't manage it. The scene before his eyes began to change. The sky was turning to Pacific blue, the sun shining, and the island emerging from the mist.

Rob resisted, and for a moment all was grey again and the view was of the back garden opposite. Garden faded into island and island into garden; for a while the picture wouldn't stabilize either way. Finally the island triumphed; it shone before him, green and golden, and the sky, blue once more, was reflected in blue water.

Rob was ashore on Welcome Beach, and his feet took him instantly to the hill on which stood the Lookout. In contrast to the last time he'd been here, the island weather was its glorious self. He was alone, happily alone, at peace alone. He didn't want animals or birds; all he wanted was endless, perfect peace.

But the happiness was brief. All wasn't well, and there couldn't be endless peace. Brightness was falling from the air and smoke hung heavily over Krakatoa. A scent of danger was in his nostrils. Before long, he knew, the volcano would erupt. And he wasn't alone on the island. There was also Dag – Dag who was weak and ill and whose means of escape he had destroyed . . .

Rob felt full of guilt, and couldn't bear it. He struggled to get away from the island, and for a moment regained his hold on the ordinary world. In the garden opposite, the man and boy were still at work, building a heap out of what they'd raked together. Rob tried once more to concentrate on the scene, to hold hard to it; but he couldn't keep the island out. He was there again, staring between the pillars of the Lookout at the ominous outline of the volcano.

'Dag!' he croaked. 'Dag! Krakatoa!' Then there was a voice crying, 'Rob! What's going on?' and he was back in the window-seat, white and shaken and with beads of sweat on his forehead. Katie was standing beside him.

'Robbie! Are you all right?'

Rob said shakily, 'Yes. Course I am.'

'You're not ill or something?'

'No, I'm not.' Then, reluctantly, 'I had a bad dream, that's all.'

'You were asleep? Sitting *there*?'

'Yes. So what? I can go to sleep where I like, can't I? It's my room. Anyway, what are you doing in it? Who asked you to come in here?'

'I wanted to talk to you about this trip to the island

with Keith. You don't want to go, do you? But you didn't answer when I knocked on the door. I knocked twice, then I came in. And Rob, did you know you were talking out loud in your sleep? You were saying something about Krakatoa.'

Rob jumped. He hadn't realized that.

'The map!' said Katie, suddenly excited. 'There was Krakatoa on the map! Rob! In your dream, did you . . . did you go to the island?'

Rob stared back at her. For a moment it was in his mind to deny it. But he couldn't. 'Maybe I did,' he said.

'That island's special to you, isn't it? All the names you made up, and the imagining you must have done for the map. And even dreaming about it!'

'Yes, well . . .'

'I *knew* that was it! I'd have done the same myself. I mean pretending and so on. You and me must be alike. I don't think I'd have dreamed about it, though. I don't dream much.'

'Lucky you!'

'Robbie! Tell me about it!'

For a moment it was on the tip of Rob's tongue to tell her to mind her own business, to order her out of his room. Then it came over him like a wave that it would be a huge relief if he could tell somebody everything.

'Well,' he said, 'it started like this . . .'

She sat down beside him, listening intently. When he'd finished, they were both silent for a minute or two. Then Rob said, 'Katie, I'm scared. At first I had to go to the lakeside and *think* myself to the island, and it was hard work. Then it got easier, and now I seem to go there without wanting to. What if it gets worse and I'm *stuck* there? And if Krakatoa blows up?'

Katie said, 'You have to get free of it, Robbie.'

'How?'

Katie was thoughtful. 'I don't know,' she said. 'Not yet, I don't. There has to be a way. But what about Keith and the real island? If you don't want to go, I'll tell him I've changed my mind and I don't want to go either. Then he'll call it off. He won't want to go there all by himself.'

'I'd never hear the end of it,' said Rob miserably. 'Keith doesn't think much of me anyway.'

'Oh, come off it, Robbie! Keith knows everybody can't be like him. But if you want to know what I think, it's that we ought to go. You shouldn't be frightened of it in real life. That wouldn't do any good.'

There was a tap on the door, and Mum came into the room. She smiled to see Rob and Katie together on the window-seat, absorbed in conversation.

'So there you both are!' she said. 'Breakfast's ready. Come and get it!'

Rob still felt reluctant to go to the real island. It crossed his mind to drop a hint to Mum about the trip. There'd certainly be ructions if she knew what Keith was planning. But he couldn't bring himself to tell. Not only would Keith and Katie despise him; he'd despise himself.

Keith had said the night before that he was going to borrow Jack Allen's van and take Rob and Katie for a ride. Pressed by Mum this morning to say where they were going, he would only tell her it was a magical mystery trip and she'd hear all about it afterwards.

'Well, mind you all come back in one piece!' she told him. 'I don't want to have to tell Rita something's happened to her daughter.'

'You don't mind if something happens to *me*?' said Rob, aggrieved.

Mum smiled and said, 'Don't look like that, pet. Of *course* I do!'

Keith said, 'Nothing's going to happen to anybody. We'll be home for dinner.'

Mum said, 'It'll be nice to have you out of the way for a bit. I can cook the Sunday dinner in peace. If Helen lets me, that is.'

Keith said, 'What are we having?'

'Roast beef and potatoes and Yorkshire pud.'

'Yum, yum,' said Keith. 'We'll come back for *that* all right!'

Keith had brought the inflatable dinghy round in the back of the van. Rob and Katie had to squeeze on to the front seat beside him. They drove past the park gates and out of town along the Rosethorn road. Then they turned left, and after half a mile or so, left again. On their left now was a long stretch of woodland, cut off from the road by a high wire fence. This was the boundary of Selhurst Park at the side away from town.

A little way along, Keith brought the van to a halt. There was a broad gate in the fence, but it was padlocked, bristling with barbed wire, and had a notice on it that said in large red capital letters DANGER − KEEP OUT − NO ADMITTANCE AT ANY TIME − BY ORDER.

'Looks like they don't want us in there,' said Katie. 'You brought your wire-cutters?'

Keith grinned. 'That's all for show,' he said. 'They know a trick or two, and so do I. Watch this.'

He went to the gate, put a hand between the bars, and fiddled with hooks and wires. The gate, still padlocked and still festooned with barbed wire, swung open.

'Not as closed as it looks,' said Keith.

He got back in the van, drove it forward through the gate, and got out again to fasten the gate behind them. Ahead, a rutted track led in among the trees. Keith drove along it, bouncing Rob and Katie up and down as the van lurched on its way. Here and there beside the track were cleared spaces, and in one of them was a pile of logs.

'This is for forestry work,' said Keith. 'Thinning out and so on.'

The track wound on, slightly downhill, for a distance that seemed greater than it was, until suddenly the lake shore came into view. Keith parked the van among trees, as close to the edge as he could get. Opposite them across the water was Pratt's Island. At first sight, from this angle, it looked unfamiliar, with everything the wrong way round. You couldn't see the boat station or the Pavilion on the mainland beyond, because the island stood exactly in the way.

'That's fine,' said Keith approvingly. 'If there's somebody on duty over there, they can't see us any more than we can see them.' He winked. 'Now help me get that thing out of the back.'

The inflatable dinghy was awkward, big and heavy. In addition, it was damp from some previous use, and none too clean. As they struggled with it, Rob and Katie soon got their clothes smeared. Keith pulled a face.

149

'We're *all* going to be in trouble with your mum,' he told Rob. 'Especially me. The trip better be worth it, eh?'

'Well, it was your idea,' said Rob. Anxiety was clenching his stomach; and it wasn't about what Mum would say.

Keith got the foot-pump from the van's spare-wheel compartment and began to work at the inflatable. It took quite a long time, but at last the dinghy began to take shape and fill out. Keith brought paddles and a couple of wooden seats out of the van.

'You two get in,' he said when he'd slotted in the seats. 'I'll push us off.' Then a thought struck him. 'Can you swim?' he inquired.

'You could have asked that before, couldn't you?' said Rob sourly. 'Yes, *I* can swim.' He added pointedly, 'My dad used to take me to the pool.'

'I can swim, too,' said Katie.

Keith took off his shoes and socks and rolled up his trousers, then pushed out the boat and leaped into it as it floated away. It tilted alarmingly as he jumped in, then righted itself but sat very low in the water.

'Not to worry,' Keith said. 'We won't get hit by a tidal wave.' He took up the paddles, and the laden dinghy moved off in a slow and stately manner towards the island. A minute later the sound of an engine, loud in the Sunday morning calm, carried across from the other side of the lake.

'What's that?' said Keith.

Rob knew. It was the outboard motor of the rescue boat. He told Keith so.

'Hell!' said Keith. 'If it comes round here, we're caught with our pants down!' He stopped paddling.

But the rescue boat didn't appear round either tip of the island. After another minute, the engine sound ceased.

'I expect they were just making sure it started,' said Keith. He began paddling again. There was a light breeze now across the water, and the little boat was tending to drift off course. Keith changed direction. It wasn't long before the dinghy bumped ashore in the little inlet on the north side of the island.

'What was your name for this, Rob?' Katie asked.

'Quicksand Bay,' said Rob.

'Mudbank Bay, more like,' said Keith. There was a dark, earthy beach, no more than three or four feet wide. Keith, still barefoot, shipped the paddles and jumped over the bow of the dinghy with the painter in his hand. Although of course it wasn't quicksand, the little beach was soft and his footprints were deep. He reached firm land, hauled up the boat, and fastened the painter to a bit of tree root, so that Katie could jump ashore without getting her feet wet.

'You now, Rob,' Keith called. But Rob stayed where he was.

'Come on, come on!' said Keith. 'What are you waiting for?'

'I – I don't want to come.'

Keith stared. 'Are you barmy?' he said. 'What are you scared of? Look, it's only a little jump. Katie did it all right. I'll catch you, anyway.'

'It's not that,' said Rob. 'I'm not bothered by a little

jump. It's . . . well, I don't want to be on the island. Not the real one.'

'What's he talking about, Katie?' Keith inquired.

'It's to do with his map,' said Katie. 'But . . .' And she shook her head, unable to explain.

Rob couldn't explain, either. But the closer they'd got to the island, the more his fear had mounted. He still hung back.

'Are you afraid somebody'll come and order us off?' Keith asked. 'You don't need to worry. If that happens, it's me that's in trouble, not you. And *I'm* not worrying.'

'It isn't that,' said Rob. 'It's . . .'

'Honestly, Rob!' said Keith, 'you make me ashamed of you. Katie's twice the lad that you are! Jump!'

He stretched out a hand. Rob, reluctantly, stood up. Grimly ignoring the hand, he jumped for the shore. The dinghy, lifting in the water as the last weight was removed from it, danced away backwards, and Rob miscalculated the leap. He landed heavily in the mud, sinking to the tops of his shoes. Keith hauled him to dry land, shaking his head but making no comment.

Rob's stomach was full of panic. He hated and feared being on the island. Pratt's Island, Paradise Island, Perilous Island. Today he felt sure it was perilous.

From somewhere in town, the Sunday morning bell-song floated towards them.

'Church time,' said Keith. 'That's where the goodies are. I guess we're the baddies. Come on, gang!'

He was grinning. 'This *really* takes me back!' he said. 'You know what? I remember the way from all those years ago. See that track there? That goes along the shore and round to the far side. And the other track goes up to the old summer-house. Let's go that way. Single file behind me!'

Keith led the way up the slope. Tangle had grown over the path, and he brushed it aside. Katie followed him, and then Rob. As they approached the round, stone-columned belvedere, Keith bent forward. 'Heads down, fellows!' he said. 'We're coming into view from the Pavilion.'

Keeping their heads low, Katie and Rob followed him to the belvedere. This was concealed by a clump of trees from the Pavilion and the boat station.

'The Lookout,' said Rob. As he spoke, he felt the change occurring. The grey autumn sky was lightening and becoming blue, the foliage around was vivid green with flowers of all hues in bloom. Pratt was becoming Paradise.

Rob fought it with all the strength of his mind. The air shimmered around him, the colour changed briefly back to grey, then wavered like a television screen barely picking up a colour transmission. He struggled to keep Paradise Island out, and for a minute or so he succeeded. Keith and Katie were still with him, and Keith was inquiring, 'The what?'

'The Lookout,' said Katie. 'That's where we are, on Rob's map. Isn't it, Rob?'

To Rob her voice sounded far away. He concentrated hard on his companions, trying to keep them with him. If he lost them, he was lost himself.

Keith was delightedly studying the row of carved initials on the parapet.

'There we are,' he said. 'KH at the top. That's me. Then DM. That was Duggie Meadows. A little thin lad he was, a shrimp you might have said, but he was tough. I don't know what happened to Duggie. Left Selhurst years ago. Then WE. That was Billy Edwards, he's still around, works for Samwells in East Street . . .'

But Keith's voice, too, was fading. Rob was looking out between the pillars of the belvedere. The pillars were wreathed in vines; the sun shone down through a burning blue sky. Over there was the other hump, the highest point of the island.

'Krakatoa,' said Rob aloud; but he wasn't speaking to anyone, for Keith and Katie had dissolved into the air.

He watched, unaware of anyone or anything but the volcano before him. It had grown since he was last on Perilous Island. From hump it had grown to hill, from hill to mountainous peak. It was still growing. It had reshaped itself to a huge black menacing cone that dominated the landscape.

It was going to erupt. That was the cause of his terror. It was going to erupt any moment. He'd always known it would erupt; and now its time had come. As he watched, a sudden great belch of smoke and flame broke out from the top of it.

Keith said – but Rob didn't hear him, for Rob was in another world – 'Christ! There's someone over there and they've lit a bonfire!'

But Rob saw billowing smoke, soaring flame, smelled the stench of burning, felt the ground shake under his feet, knew the eruption had begun and would be fast and violent. And in Skull Cave, under the cliffs on the farther slope of Krakatoa, was Dag; Dag whom he'd imprisoned.

Rob leaped from the Lookout and was running, running, as hard as he could go, round the base of Krakatoa towards the cliffs of Sheer Head. There were great lumps of burning debris blackening the air all round him, and there was molten lava flowing after him, chasing him, and he had to save Dag. He was running, running, running, and he was at the cliff top, and he had to scramble down it to the cave, but he couldn't because there was no foothold, and he was falling, sliding, falling, down and down the cliff and into the Pacific Ocean.

The water of Selhurst Lake.

13

He was in the water, and the water was in him, and he couldn't get up, he couldn't do anything, he could only drown.

Rob was unconscious. Then he was conscious again, and he was upside down, and Keith, standing in the water, had him by the ankles. Katie was holding his head back by the hair, and his back was being thumped and everything hurt and he was trying desperately to draw breath and the breath wouldn't come and he was still drowning and he was unconscious again.

He was conscious once more and he was on the ground and Keith's mouth was pressed against his and water was being vacuumed out of him. And then he was breathing – painfully, chokingly, with enormous effort, but breathing.

There was the sound of an engine and there was the rescue boat close by and there were four people grouped round him on the shore and one of them was his old friend, the former boat attendant, Mike. And the world was the real world and he was alive in it, though he hadn't the strength to do anything but struggle for still-precious breath. He wanted all the breath there was, and it still wouldn't be enough.

Mike was bending over him and saying, 'Christ, it's young Rob! How did he get here?'

Then Mike was calling Keith a bloody fool and telling him it was almost a tragedy and it was all his fault, and Keith was taking it and not even answering back.

Then Rob was sitting, white-faced and still weak, in the rescue boat, and Katie was beside him and had her arms round him and was saying, 'It's all right, Robbie, it's all *right*,' and Keith wasn't there and Mike was at the tiller and the rescue boat was heading for the landing-stage.

Then he was in the Pavilion, drinking hot sweet tea. Then he was in somebody's car. Then he was at home, lying on the sofa, and all sorts of people were trying to tell Mum what had happened, and he could hear Helen crying, and nobody was taking any notice of her. Then he was being tucked up in bed, and he was warm and comfortable and sleepy. Then he was asleep. And then he was awake, and Keith was there, sitting on the bed.

Keith asked in bewilderment, 'What *made* you run away like that and jump in the lake as if all hell was after you? What *was* it, Rob? Was it something *I* said or did?'

As Keith spoke, Rob's mind took a sudden lurch and he was on the island again. The volcano had stopped erupting, but there was lava and ash everywhere, and choking fumes, and the air was thick with particles, and it seemed there could be nothing alive except himself. And he hadn't saved Dag . . .

He dragged himself back into the real world, though the island still lingered close by, somewhere in the shadows. Keith was sitting on the bed beside him, looking at him with troubled eyes. Rob was frightened, but he didn't know how to tell Keith what was happening, and he didn't want to sound crazy.

'It – it just came over me,' he said. 'I felt like running, after being cooped up in the boat. I didn't realize it was so little distance to the edge.'

'You gave us the fright of our lives, Rob,' said Keith. 'We thought we'd lost you for good.'

Rob concentrated his attention on Keith, and the island drew back from the borders of his mind. He was firmly in the real world. 'What happened to the boat?' he asked.

'The dinghy? Oh, I paddled it back and let it down and got it into the van somehow. Hell of a struggle it was. I drove it back to Trev Norris. Can't tell you how glad I was to be rid of it. That was a real bad idea of mine, Rob. I guess I can't be eleven years old again at *my* age. Funny that it should be your pal Mike who was on the island lighting that bonfire. He gets weekend work in the park sometimes while he's at Selhurst Poly. He says I'll get a bill for ten pounds' fine, and cheap at the price. As for what your mum said to me, well, I won't repeat it. Rob, old fellow, my name's M–U–D from now on.'

'Not with me it isn't,' said Rob. Suddenly, for the first time ever, he felt fond of Keith. 'I'm sorry I gave you a bad time,' he said.

'Well,' said Keith, 'if you and me's pals, there's good come out of it all. Shake, friend.'

He held out a large, warm hand. Rob shook it.

But at night, the island came back and invaded his mind again. Time after time, as the hours went sleeplessly past, he found himself wandering hopelessly in the charred desolation of his one-time paradise, wretched with guilt because he hadn't saved Dag. Dawn light was seeping through his curtains, and the outlines of his bed-room furniture were becoming visible, when he fell at last into uneasy sleep.

An hour or so later Katie, passing Rob's door on her way to the bathroom, heard sighs and groans, and went into his room to see if he was all right. She leaned over the bed. Rob half-woke, stared up at her, and said in a voice full of agony, 'He's underneath it all. He couldn't escape. It was all my fault!'

'There, there, Robbie! You've been dreaming again! It's morning now. There's nothing wrong.'

Rob was wide awake at once.

'There is!' he said. 'I'm scared, Katie. I think I'm bonkers. What if they put me away?'

'*Course* you're not bonkers!' Katie said.

'You and Keith must have thought I was crazy when I ran off and jumped in the lake.'

Katie said, 'You ever heard of stress, Rob? That's what it was. Stress. I heard your mum and Keith say so.'

'Yes. But. You see, maybe I *am* crazy. And why I'm scared is, I found myself on the island – I mean the map island, the imaginary island – when I wasn't trying. *That's* why I ran and fell in the water. The volcano had erupted all over everything, and Dag – that's the castaway that I told you about – was underneath it all, and I had to get him out, but I couldn't.'

'Sounds like a nightmare, except it was in the daytime,' said Katie.

'Yes, but that's not all. I keep on going there, in my

159

mind, although I try not to. What if I get *stuck* there, Katie, for ever and ever? *Then* I'll be bonkers, won't I?'

Katie was silent for a while. Then she said, 'I think you've got to go there again on purpose, just once more. You've got to rescue this person. Then you'll be *able* to leave the island. It won't be on your mind like it is now. It'll be finished.'

'But I don't want to go again. Not even once. That's what I'm scared of. And I don't think I *can* rescue Dag. All the time I'm there, I feel as if I can't. There's something stopping me, and I don't know what it is.'

Katie said, 'You're going again, Rob, and I'm coming with you. I won't *let* you get stuck, and I bet we *can* rescue Dag. Rob's Last Voyage, that's what it'll be. The end of the story.'

'What makes you think you *could* go?'

'If you can, I bet *I* can. Didn't I tell you we're alike? *Course* I can do it. Just tell me how.'

Rob said, 'It seems to happen to *me* anywhere, now. But it was quite hard at first. Might be best to go where I went, down by the lake, with the island right there opposite you, where you can see it.'

'All right. Let's go. Now, while it's still early and they're all in bed.'

'I don't think I ought to start you doing it,' Rob said. 'Look at the mess it's got *me* into.'

'Don't argue, Rob. Just get dressed, and I'll go and do the same, and I'll leave a note for your mum to say we'll be back soon. And then we're on our way!'

It was a dismal day: not wet, exactly, but moist, with a

wisp of mist. They ran all the way to the park, in through the gates, and down the grass slope to the parking lot. At this time of day there were no cars parked there at all. Rob led the way through the gap in the hedge to the spot beneath the beech tree. Other trees around had mostly lost their leaves, but the beech leaves, crisp and brown, were still on the tree.

'This is where I used to go from,' Rob explained. 'First, you climb on that long overhanging branch. Can you do that?'

'Course I can. Dead easy.' Katie scrambled up. 'Now what?'

Rob climbed up beside her.

'Well, the first time I ever went, with Mike, we imagined a yacht and sailed to the island in it.'

'All right, then, Robbie. We've got a yacht. What's she called?'

'You name her,' said Rob.

'I name her ... I name her ... *Sundancer*. How's that?'

'Sounds fine to me.'

'What do we do next?'

Rob tried to recall his voyage with Mike.

'We're on board now,' he told her. 'You can feel the movement.' He rocked the branch slightly. 'Now look up. See the sails overhead?'

'Yes. Smashing white, aren't they, like laundry? I mean, well, white and gleaming. And the sky as blue as blue.'

'You've got the idea!' said Rob.

Katie rocked the branch more vigorously. 'We're out

on the ocean deep,' she said. 'There's some that would be seasick, but not us!'

'Careful!' said Rob. 'No storms! We don't want to fall off – I mean in. Food for the sharks.'

'It was just a squall,' said Katie.

For Rob the transformation began to work once more. As Katie spoke, the branches overhead became sails, the sky changed from grey to cloudless blue, and he was warm all over from the tropical sun.

'We got a fair wind, I reckon,' said Katie. 'That's what they call it when the wind's behind you, isn't it? How many knots are we doing, Robbie?'

'Ten or twelve at least. Fifteen, maybe.'

'Terrific. Now, what's that on the horizon?' Katie shaded her eyes with her hand. 'Looks like an island to me. Paradise Island!'

Rob was in the island world now; he couldn't have got out of it if he'd wanted. But he was full of anxiety. He was eager to arrive, eager to see if he could still rescue Dag. And at the same time he didn't want to get there at all, because he was afraid.

'It's Perilous Island!' he said.

'Same thing,' said Katie. '"The Island with Two Names", the sailors call it. Most beautiful island in the Pacific!'

'But dangerous!' said Rob.

'We're not frightened, shipmate. We can deal with dangers.'

'Can we?' said Rob; and then, 'The wind's dropped. We're becalmed.'

'We're not. We're still moving. Look at the wake!'

'We're *becalmed*!' Rob insisted. 'We won't get there! I'm the skipper, and I'm telling you, we won't make it!' He still didn't know whether it would be agony or relief if they didn't get to the island.

'Robbie, we will! We *got* to make it!'

'There's no wind,' said Rob. 'Not a breath!'

'There is, Rob, there is. Look, the sails are filling. There's wind behind us. Can't you feel it? And the ship's moving. Can't you feel *that*?'

Rob felt breath on his cheek, which must be the wind, and motion beneath him, which must be the boat.

'Yes,' he admitted. 'Yes, we're moving.'

'You're the skipper, but I'm the helmsman,' said Katie, 'and we're doing fine. Now we have to tack, to get to our anchorage. The wind's rising, and we're heeling over quite a bit. Can't you feel us heeling over?'

Rob could feel the boat heeling over.

'We're moving *fast*!' Katie said. 'Getting near land, now. We'll have to go about and head into the wind. Time to drop anchor. That's right. Well done, shipmate. Here we are, riding at anchor, nice and comfortable. Now I'll row you ashore in the ship's dinghy. Away we go!'

Rob said, 'You have your back to the island, rowing. *I* can see forward. And Krakatoa *did* erupt. There's lava and ash all over. Nothing else.'

Katie said, 'I bet you're wrong, Rob. We're ashore now. We'll head up the beach and take a closer look. Yes, I knew you were wrong. There's green shoots coming through everywhere. Things are growing like mad. You can almost see them growing. Trees and flowers and everything! Now, where's your cabin?'

'Burned down, what was left of it.'

'It wasn't burned down. I can see its roof. It was spared, Rob. Miraculously spared. And it's not in bad condition at all. Good as new, nearly.'

Rob said, 'Hey, whose island *is* this?'

Katie said. 'It's yours, Rob. And everything's going to be all right. Now, what about your animal friends? Can we find them?'

'We've got to look for Dag,' Rab said. 'In the cave.'

'We may need help. There was a dog, wasn't there? What's his name?'

'Crusoe.'

'Call him, Rob.'

Rob called, 'Crusoe! Crusoe!' Then he said, 'He hasn't come. Maybe he . . . didn't survive.'

'Course he survived! You didn't call him loudly enough, that's all. Try again. Whistle!'

Rob put two fingers to his mouth and whistled loudly.

'Here he comes!' said Katie. 'Running up to us. I knew he'd be around. Good boy, Crusoe. There, isn't he glad to see you, Rob? And he looks fine and healthy, doesn't he?'

Rob stroked Crusoe's head. It was a long time since they'd been together. But Crusoe seemed to have managed pretty well without him.

'I guess he's all right,' he said. 'He hasn't missed me.'

'And the parrot,' said Katie. 'What's *his* name? Captain Flint, is it?'

'No, it's Billy Bones.'

'*I'll* call him. Billy Bones! Billy Bo – ones!'

164

A voice squawked in Rob's ear, 'Hello, Rob, how are you?'

'What else does he say, Rob?' Katie asked.

'He says "Gold moidores, Spanish doubloons",' said Rob.

'Spanish doubloons! Gold moidores!' squawked the voice in Rob's ear.

'Well, that's two of them that are all right,' Katie said. 'And then there's the leopard . . .'

'The puma,' Rob corrected her.

'Sorry. I don't know how you call a puma.'

'I don't call him. He just comes, if he wants to. He lives over in the Black Forest. We have to go that way, to get to Skull Cave. And we'd better hurry!' Now the quest was under way, Rob was suddenly eager to get on with it.

'What if we had digging-out to do?' said Katie. 'We need a pickaxe and a spade. Here they are, in the corner of the cabin. Off we go, Robbie. You'd better point things out to me as we go, so I'll know where we are.'

'This is the Wilderness we're going through now,' Rob said. 'And now on the right there's Quicksand Bay. We cross the Hanging Bridge here, over Deep Gorge.'

'Makes me feel dizzy, Rob.'

'You haven't time to be dizzy. Now we go due west to Sheer Head. Takes us through the Black Forest.'

'Here we go now, among the trees. It isn't much of a track, is it, but Crusoe seems to know the way. And look at Billy Bones, fluttering from branch to branch. And, Robbie, I can see the puma!'

'We haven't time to stop for him.'

'I think we'll need him. That's him, isn't it, in that tree, lying along a branch?'

'Yes, that's him,' said Rob reluctantly.

'He's coming down off the branch. He's glad to see you, Rob. Rubbing the side of his head against you, like a great big cat!'

Rob stroked the puma, but only for a moment. Then he said, 'Come on. We're out of the forest now. This is Sheer Head.'

'And Skull Cave's at the bottom of the cliff. That's right, isn't it? We must find a way down. There's a path, Robbie. You lead the way. Mind you don't slip.'

'We're coming to Skull Cave now,' said Rob.

'And it's *not* covered in lava!' said Katie instantly.

'No. But there's mud and rocks and stuff that came down in the eruption. The opening's buried under it. Buried deep.'

'Yes. Good job we brought the pickaxe and spade.'

'We don't know where to start digging. Or how far we'll have to go. Or whether he'll still be alive. I'm scared, Katie. I'm scared he'll be dead.'

'Course he won't be dead. And we'll find where to start. Crusoe! Crusoe! Sniff him out, boy! See, Rob? Crusoe's running up and down, looking for the place. He'll soon find it. There, what did I tell you? He's showing us, as plain as if he could talk, where to start digging. You take the pick and I'll take the spade.'

Rob felt pessimistic again. He said, 'We'll dig for ever and get nowhere.'

Katie said, 'Keep going!'

Rob said, 'We've been digging for hours. Days. We're exhausted. This isn't going to work.'

'It *is* going to work. Look, Crusoe's digging as well. *And* the puma. Scratching away and throwing the mud back.'

'Pumas don't dig.'

'How do you know they don't? This one's digging. And look, we've got down to some boulders, and there's an opening between them. That must lead somewhere.'

'It's only a *little* opening,' said Rob.

'We'll send Billy Bones in through it. Hey, Billy Bones!'

Billy Bones squawked in Rob's ear, 'Here I am!'

Rob was hopeful again.

'Go and find Dag, Billy Bones!' he said.

Billy Bones fluttered in through the opening. Rob and Katie waited. From somewhere underground they thought they heard a distant voice. A minute later, Billy Bones reappeared. 'Dag!' he squawked in Rob's ear. 'Found Dag!'

The rescuers dug faster, until there was an opening that Rob and Katie could climb through. Inside, all was dark except for a shaft of light that came in through the gap they'd just made.

'We brought a torch,' Katie said. '*Course* we brought a torch. There was one in the cabin.'

'You don't find electric torches on South Sea islands,' objected Rob.

'Don't be picky. This one has long-life batteries. Look, it's working fine.'

They moved cautiously through the darkness, flashing the torch ahead of them. Before long, Rob heard a croaking sound: 'Rob, is that you? Get me out of here!'

'Coming, Dad! I mean Dag!' called Rob. They groped their way through a vast cavern until, guided by his feeble voice, they found Dag lying in a corner.

'You are just in time to save my life!' he gasped; and then, 'Help me. I am too weak to move.'

'We must get him into the open,' Rob said. Between them, they dragged Dag to where a tiny shaft of light shone in from outside. Katie climbed up through the opening. Rob managed to push Dag through to a point where Katie could grasp his shoulders and heave him into the daylight.

The animals gathered round. Crusoe licked Dag's face. Katie said to Billy Bones, 'Where's the nearest water?' Billy Bones squawked, 'This way!' and led her to a tiny spring. A half coconut shell lay near by, and Katie carried water to the rescued man, who sipped it gratefully.

Katie whispered to Rob, 'Now you must tell him what you did.'

Rob said, 'I'm sorry, Dag, that I broke up your boat and made it impossible for you to leave the island. I won't keep you any more. We shall take you to the cabin, where there is food, and you can rest until you are well. And we shall leave *our* boat in the inlet. You can go wherever in the world you want to go!'

They said farewell to the puma, and Dag, who was stronger already, made his way along the trail to the cabin, leaning on Rob's and Katie's shoulders. There he lay down to rest. Rob said to Katie, 'What about us?'

Katie said, 'We're going back to the mainland, aren't we?'

Rob said, 'Yes. Yes, of course we are.' And with a sense of huge relief he knew he was free to go.

He and Dag hugged each other. Dag said, 'We are not parting for ever. We shall meet again in other climes, and be closer than before.'

And so Rob and Katie left the cabin. Outside, Rob said, 'I shall miss the animals.'

Katie said, 'I expect they'll miss *you*. But they'll be all right. They were all right on their own before.'

Crusoe looked at Rob soulfully, then raised a paw and solemnly shook hands with him. Billy Bones squawked, 'Goodbye, Rob. Goodbye, Katie. Good luck!' And Crusoe and Billy Bones disappeared for ever into the Wilderness.

Katie said, 'Well now, Rob, all we've got to do is get back to *Sundancer* and sail to the mainland. Come on.'

They stood by the shore. Rob said, 'We haven't a dinghy to get back to the yacht. We promised to leave it for Dag.'

Katie said, 'Oh, well, we can swim out to the yacht.'

Rob said, 'But what about sharks?' And then, as he looked out from the shore of Paradise Island, the yacht, riding handsomely at anchor, began to dissolve before his eyes. Sky and water were fading from blue to grey.

'Sharks?' he said. 'What sharks? There aren't any sharks here.'

There were branches around him. Long, horizontal branches, with brown beech leaves clinging to them. Everything was the other way round, and he wasn't looking out from the island, he was looking towards it, and it was small and green and familiar. It was Pratt's Island. There was a girl in jeans sitting beside him, and their eyes met. Katie said, 'Are you here, Rob? With me? Sitting in the tree?'

'Yes, I'm here,' said Rob. 'In Selhurst.'

'You got safely away, then.'

Rob said, 'It wasn't real. It was only a game.'

Katie said, 'I don't know. It was only *partly* a game. We had to do it.'

Rob said, 'I'm on the mainland now, Katie. I've finished with the island. Paradise or Perilous, I don't care which you call it. I won't need to go there again, ever.'

Katie said, 'Well, not if you don't want.'

Rob said, 'I don't think I'll ever want.'

Katie said, 'All right, Robbie. Jump down off the branch.'

Rob jumped down from the beech tree and landed firmly on the solid ground beneath. Katie followed. Hand in hand, they ran together across the grass of Selhurst Park and along the road to the house where Mum and Keith and the baby were waiting.

Mum was cross at first, for about half a minute. 'The pair of you, going off like that, first thing in the morning!' she said. 'And Rob after an experience like he had yesterday!'

Rob said, 'I'm all right. I feel fine. We had a great time. And I'm hungry. Is breakfast ready?'

Mum said, 'Well, I must say, you look all right. And, Rob Little, you're *smiling*! That's a change. I can't remember when I last saw you smile. What's happened?'

Katie said, '*I've* happened!'

14

Keith had a day off, and for Rob and Katie it was still half-term. All three of them spent the first half of Monday morning planning a tree-house, to be built in one of the apple trees next time Katie was in Selhurst. They squabbled a good deal over the design. Then they went for a walk in the park. Katie and Rob fooled about, chasing each other and dodging round Keith and the pram. For the first time in months, Rob was in a skittish mood. He felt lighthearted and a bit silly.

The boats had been put away for the winter, but the door of the boathouse was open, and as they went past Mike came out.

'Hi, Rob!' he said. 'How you feeling?'

'Terrific!'

'You look all right. But when I think what might have happened . . .' He frowned and said to Keith, 'I don't know how you have the cheek to bring them here so soon afterwards.'

Keith grinned, a little shamefacedly. Mike said, 'I called you a bloody fool yesterday.'

Keith said, 'Yes. You're the only person who's ever done that and lived.'

Mike said, 'I'll call you it again today. You're a bloody fool. I hope you've learned a bit of sense.'

Keith said, 'I might still crunch you up for that. I

172

could, you know. I could eat you for breakfast, Mike Tisdall, and still have room for toast.' He put on a ferocious expression. Then he grinned again and said, 'However, maybe I won't. Not this time, anyway.'

Farther along the path, Keith said, 'Well, there's your island. Fancy another trip?'

Rob said, 'No, thank you.'

Keith said, 'Maybe at ten pounds a throw it's too expensive.'

Rob looked across the water at Pratt's Island. The sky was grey again, the atmosphere damp. The trees had lost nearly all their leaves. It was just a nondescript patch of bumpy land – a few scruffy trees and bushes, a store shed, an abandoned summer-house, and weed and grass and reed. For the time being at least, it had lost its charm for him. 'I'm just not interested,' he said.

Later, Keith and Rob walked Katie to the bus station. Keith kissed Katie heartily and told her to come again. Rob and Katie scuffled while they waited for the coach, and shouted farewell insults at each other as Katie went on board. She got a back seat and pulled faces at them through the rear window until the coach left.

On the way home, Keith said to Rob, 'She's a great kid.'

Rob said, 'She's all right.'

Keith said, 'Well, I suppose that's praise, coming from you.'

Mum was setting the table for supper. Helen was awake and propped up in her carry-cot. Her eyes followed Rob as he moved around. He went over to her and practised some faces to pull at Katie next time he saw her. Helen grinned and gurgled.

Rob said, 'She's sharp, isn't she? I mean, she doesn't miss anything that's going on.'

Mum said, 'She's an *interesting* baby. Babies *are* interesting.'

Rob said, 'Yes. Well. Maybe. If only she didn't keep bawling . . .'

Mum said, 'Babies do cry.' She added, hopefully, 'She doesn't cry as much as she used to do, does she? Well, not *quite* as much. At least, I *think* not.'

After supper, Keith went to wash the dishes. Rob's offer of help was declined with thanks. 'You go talk to your mum,' Keith said.

Helen was on Mum's lap, being fed some gooey mess, most of which ended on the outside of her mouth.

'It's her first solid food,' said Mum. It didn't look very solid to Rob.

Rob said thoughtfully, 'Katie asked me today what my school was like.'

'And what did you tell her?'

'I said it's all right. Well, I suppose it's all right. All the kids say it's better than Bright Street. But why does she want to know?'

Mum didn't say anything to that. Rob went on, 'I wonder if she thinks she might go there.'

Mum said, very slowly, 'Well, I suppose she might.'

Rob said, 'I know what that means.'

Mum said, 'Do you, Robbie?'

Rob said, 'Yes. If Dad gets that job in Selhurst, Katie and her mum might come too.'

'Yes, that's possible, Rob.'

'And Dad and Rita might get married.'

Once again, Mum didn't say anything. Rob asked, 'If they did, would I go and live with them?'

Mum said, 'I think it would be up to you. I expect the court would let you live with whichever you wanted. Why, Rob? Which do you think you *would* want?'

Rob said, 'I don't know. It might be hard to decide.' He paused. 'You know what Dad promised me.'

Keith had come in from the kitchen. He had a cup in one hand and a tea-towel in the other. He and Mum looked at each other. Mum had a spoonful of Helen's goo in her hand, but just for the moment she wasn't attending to Helen. She said, 'Yes, I know what your dad promised, and you know what I think about it. He shouldn't have made a promise like that.'

For a moment, Rob felt his distress coming back. Dad was the one person in the world who had put him first. He'd needed somebody to put him first. If Dad remarried, Rob wouldn't come first any more. Not in the same way. That would take some getting used to. But . . .

'I wouldn't hold him to it,' he said.

Keith dropped the teacup, and swore. Then, without stopping to pick up the pieces, he strode over to Rob and slapped him on the back.

'There's my lad!' he said with approval. 'Dead right!'

'Anyway,' said Rob, 'Dad only said he wouldn't get married if I hated it. It'd be different if I didn't mind.' He added slowly, 'Maybe I wouldn't mind.'

Mum asked, 'May I tell your dad that?'

'No,' said Rob, 'I'll tell him it myself.'

Just for a moment there flashed into his mind a last picture of his island. The castaway Dag, fit and recovered, was striding across to the inlet to pick up the boat that Rob and Katie had left for him. He was free to go where he wished and do what he wanted to do; and in freeing him Rob had freed himself. The world was before them both.

Keith said, 'Two homes to choose from, and I bet you'll choose them both! Some folks are born lucky, young Rob, and I reckon you're one of them. Now fetch a dustpan and help me pick up these pieces!'